"Goodnight, Samantha Reese.

His voice was low, sexy, drawing out the syllables of her name in a rumbling tone. Dazed and breathless, she realized he'd used her full name. Samantha. No more Dr. Kearn; she was Samantha, now. "See you tomorrow."

Speechless, she could only stare after him as he turned and ambled away. Realizing she was standing with the door wide open, staring down an empty hallway, she quickly closed and locked it, then leaned against the wood, her head tilted back against the door, her heart beating rapidly in her chest.

Reese wasn't a part of her master plan, but somehow she suspected he wasn't going to be easy to ignore.

And the thought brought a thrill of anticipation she hadn't experienced in years…

AIR RESCUE

High-flying doctors—

High-altitude medical drama

**Look out for more AIR RESCUE novels and
Laura Iding's next LIFELINE story,
THE FLIGHT DOCTOR'S EMERGENCY
coming in September 2005
from Mills & Boon® Medical Romance™**

THE FLIGHT DOCTOR'S LIFELINE

BY
LAURA IDING

MILLS & BOON

To my sister Michele, thanks for all your
support and encouragement. I love you.

DID YOU PURCHASE THIS BOOK WITHOUT A COVER?

If you did, you should be aware it is **stolen property** as it was reported
unsold and destroyed by a retailer. Neither the author nor the publisher
has received any payment for this book.

*All the characters in this book have no existence outside the imagination
of the author, and have no relation whatsoever to anyone bearing the
same name or names. They are not even distantly inspired by any
individual known or unknown to the author, and all the incidents are
pure invention.*

*All Rights Reserved including the right of reproduction in whole or in
part in any form. This edition is published by arrangement with
Harlequin Enterprises II B.V. The text of this publication or any part
thereof may not be reproduced or transmitted in any form or by any
means, electronic or mechanical, including photocopying, recording,
storage in an information retrieval system, or otherwise, without the
written permission of the publisher.*

*This book is sold subject to the condition that it shall not, by way of
trade or otherwise, be lent, resold, hired out or otherwise circulated
without the prior consent of the publisher in any form of binding or
cover other than that in which it is published and without a similar
condition including this condition being imposed on the subsequent
purchaser.*

*MILLS & BOON and MILLS & BOON with the Rose Device
are registered trademarks of the publisher.*

*First published in Great Britain 2005
Harlequin Mills & Boon Limited,
Eton House, 18-24 Paradise Road, Richmond, Surrey TW9 1SR*

© Laura Iding 2005

ISBN 0 263 84319 X

*Set in Times Roman 10½ on 12½ pt.
03-0705-41900*

*Printed and bound in Spain
by Litografia Rosés, S.A., Barcelona*

CHAPTER ONE

"Two minutes till landing."

Dr Samantha Kearn took a deep breath as Reese Jarvis's calm, steady voice flowed through her headset. The Lifeline helicopter pilot could have made a living as a radio announcer playing late-night love songs. His voice reminded her of hot, sultry nights, in contrast to the harsh, cold winter day she was stuck flying in.

At least she was flying.

This was it. Her first solo flight as the physician in charge. Reese landed the helicopter gently, without so much as a thud. For a moment she hesitated, her hand on the door. What if she messed up? Then with a sudden burst of determination she pushed the door open and jumped to the ground. She wouldn't screw up. She was confident in her training. And maybe she was finally putting her past behind her, too. With renewed vigor, she followed Andrew, the flight paramedic on board, and helped him slide the gurney through the hatch in the back of the chopper.

Samantha's sweeping glance gauged the distance from the helicopter to the building. The small community hospital didn't have a rooftop helipad—they would be forced to cross the expansive and mostly empty surface parking lot to find the hospital entrance and then finally the intensive care unit.

She'd already gotten a brief report. Her patient was Jamie Armon, a thirty-eight-year-old woman who had originally come in with flu-like symptoms which had grown increasingly worse over the next several days, hence the request to airlift her to a larger, tertiary care hospital. Samantha frowned as they rode the elevator to the third floor. What she needed was an update on Jamie's condition.

Inside the hospital's small ICU, her first glance at the monitor over the patient's bedside made her heart sink. As a rule, patients needed to be stable prior to transport, but right now Jamie teetered on the edge, seeming ready to free-fall to the bottom of a deep canyon. Samantha firmed her resolve. No way was she going to lose her patient on her first solo flight.

"How much dopamine do you have her on?" she asked the nurse as Andrew began to switch all the IV connections to their smaller, compact transport models.

"I'm not sure. Around 7 micrograms per kilo per minute, I think." The Cedar Ridge Hospital nurse appeared flustered as she gathered the chart and thrust the stack of paperwork at Andrew.

Samantha felt a flash of pity. Smaller community hospitals didn't see complicated patients every day and if the nurse wasn't getting support from the physicians, no wonder she was frazzled.

"Let me see." Samantha looked at the bag for the dose, then at the pump for the rate. She quickly did the math and figured the patient was getting at least twice that much. "She's on much higher doses than what I was told. Has her blood pressure always been that low?"

"Yeah. No matter how high I titrate the medication, she doesn't get any better. The doctors here aren't even sure what's wrong with her." The nurse's bloodshot eyes were wide with anxiety.

"Let me see her labs." Samantha took the paperwork from Andrew's unresisting fingers. Leafing through the information, she found what she was looking for. "From what I see, she can afford more volume. Increase her fluids. Also, her potassium is low, so hang a supplement before we go. Do you have all her radiology films in here?"

"Yes. The most recent chest X-ray is on top. We took it about ten minutes ago after putting a new central line in."

A new line? Samantha filed that bit of news away. "All right, let's go." Samantha nodded at Andrew. There wasn't much more they could do other than get Jamie to Trinity Medical Center as soon as possible.

They packed Jamie up and wheeled her out to the waiting chopper. The wind was bitterly cold as they crossed the parking lot, and Samantha tugged the blanket tighter around their patient. The goal was always to get in and out of the hospital within twenty minutes and they'd barely made it. Reese had kept the helicopter running, ready for takeoff.

With Andrew's help, she loaded the patient and then climbed in after her. Andrew shut the hatch behind them. As soon as they were buckled safely inside, Reese asked, "Are you ready back there?"

"We're good to go," Samantha confirmed, before

placing the extra pair of headphones on Jamie's head so they could communicate, although the woman was pretty out of it. Even as she watched, Jamie's blood pressure dipped lower.

Reese was conversing with local air traffic control, giving coordinates for their flight plan, so she waited until he was finished.

"Reese, what's the fastest you can get us to Trinity?" As she spoke, she increased the dopamine. The medication was nearly maxed out. The knot in her belly tightened. If her patient's pressure didn't get better, she'd have to add another vasopresser.

"We have the north wind behind us now so should be able to make it back to Milwaukee in forty-five minutes. There's light snow beginning to fall, though. I might have to fly at a lower altitude to avoid freezing rain, adding time to the trip."

Normally, the idea of flying in freezing rain bothered her. She'd learned in her training how ice coating the blades could down a chopper faster than a clay pigeon. But Reese's voice was so unflappably steady, she didn't argue. "Do what you can to get us to Trinity as soon as possible."

"Hey, Dr Kearn, I'm not feeling a pulse here," Andrew interjected, holding his fingers on Jamie's carotid.

Samantha mentally swore as the patient's blood pressure dropped even lower. She pulled the blankets aside and noticed the skin along the entire left side of the patient's chest, the side with the new line, looked puffy. Just then the chopper took a hard bump. Since she was unbelted and perched on the edge of the bench seat, Samantha almost fell face-first onto her patient.

"Sorry, are you all right back there?" Reese's even tone eased her alarm, calming her shaky nerves.

"Yes, but we have a problem. She's crashing. Can you hold this thing steady?" Samantha asked.

"If I need to slow down and lower my altitude, I will," was his immediate response.

"I need to insert a small chest tube because I think she has a tension pneumothorax." Samantha quickly dug in the flight bag for the necessary equipment. Maybe she should have waited before transporting the patient.

"Now?" Andrew's voice rose an octave. "A chest tube? I've never done an in-flight chest tube."

"Watch closely, then, because we're doing one now." Samantha didn't let on how she'd only performed the procedure a half-dozen times herself. And never thousands of feet in the air.

"Okay, I'm reducing altitude," Reese informed them.

The helicopter's flight smoothed out. Samantha took a large-bore needle and catheter and quickly jabbed the instrument between the woman's ribs. Jamie moaned and flinched beneath her hands. Andrew managed to connect the small portable suction machine to the catheter end.

"I have a pulse." Samantha couldn't prevent the wave of relief. Thank goodness, the chest tube worked.

"Blood pressure is up—98 over 50." Andrew sounded relieved as he sat back in his seat.

Reese banked the helicopter, heading into the wind. This time Samantha anticipated the move and managed to keep her balance.

"Do you need me to divert to another facility?" Reese asked a few minutes later.

To veer off course and request an emergency standby landing was rare. Most pilots would rather push on to the scheduled destination. She wasn't surprised to discover Reese was the kind of pilot to do whatever was best for their patient.

"No, thanks. I think we can make it to Trinity." Samantha busied her hands with double-checking everything, hiding the fact that she was shaking. She wondered if Andrew had any idea how close their patient had come to dying.

"ETA twenty minutes, then." Reese's steady voice surrounded her, filling her helmet. "Just let me know if you need anything. I'm going to climb back up another five hundred feet."

"Uh-oh, her pressure's dropping again." Andrew's tone betrayed his concern.

"I'm going to start another line. I'm not convinced the one they placed is any good." Samantha quickly prepared the site.

"Do you want to take a look at this chest X-ray?" Andrew held up the film, using the light from the window as a backdrop to sharpen the image.

"Yeah." Samantha peered at the image. At first glance, it looked fine. Then she narrowed her gaze and leaned closer. Sure enough, if you looked close enough, you could just barely see how the very tip of the line went through the vein. "Thanks, that's all I need."

"Dr Kearn, do you need me to reduce altitude again?"

She was surprised to hear Reese address her so formally, but she was thankful he was paying attention to what was going on with her patient. The situation was still tenuous, but his reassuring voice remained her anchor.

"If you could." Somewhere along the way, her fingers had stopped shaking and she was able to insert the needle and find the subclavian vein without difficulty. *That's it*, she told herself. *Just pretend you're in the ED where you completed months of training. See? No problem.*

Within a few minutes she had the new line placed.

"Connect the drips, I have good blood flow. The chest X-ray will have to wait until we land at Trinity," Samantha told Andrew.

Moments later, her patient's blood pressure responded beautifully. Satisfied, Samantha quickly cleaned and dressed the site.

"ETA eight minutes. Less if I put more air under our belly. There's a nice tailwind up there."

The image of Reese bodysurfing, flying like Superman on a wave of wind, almost made Samantha laugh out loud. Now that the worst of the danger was over, she could afford to relax. Reese was seated up front and couldn't see her, but she grinned anyway.

"Sure, why not? I like a little air under my belly. And things are better back here."

Andrew quickly made several notations on the clipboard, reducing the rate of the dopamine drip. With the line working properly, the patient didn't need nearly as high a dose.

"Five minutes until landing."

Samantha didn't respond. Instead, she helped Andrew get their patient prepared for transport. She hit the button on her mike, signaling a call to the paramedic base. "Lifeline to paramedic base, please let Trinity's ICU know the patient is on lower dose of dopamine than that reported earlier. Also, request a portable X-ray machine on standby to verify central line placement."

"Roger, Lifeline."

Reese landed the helicopter with finesse on the rooftop helipad at Trinity Medical Center. Samantha waited until he gave her the all-clear to unload her patient.

Andrew helped wheel the gurney through the automatic doors and into the trauma elevator. As the only level-one trauma center in the area, Lifeline staff often took patients to Trinity, so the route was a familiar one. The elevator took them all the way down to the fourth-floor ICU.

As promised, the portable X-ray machine was ready and waiting. The X-ray proved the central line she'd placed en route was good, and it verified the tension pneumothorax was almost completely resolved. Relieved, Samantha watched the ICU team work on Jamie, a woman only eight years her senior. Now that she'd handed over Jamie's care, the seriousness of the situation hit hard. This poor young woman had almost died up there. Thank heavens she'd recognized the problems early enough to fix them.

"Nice job, Dr Kearn. Ready to go?"

"Yeah." She really wasn't, but regretfully turned anyway and helped Andrew wheel the now empty gurney back to the elevator. She'd survived her first solo flight. Surely the flights would get easier from here on out. Now, if she could only find a way to get the rest of her personal life on track. *One step at a time*, she reminded herself. *You have a new apartment and you're in the last four months of your training. You finally have your independence. Be thankful for what you have.*

Once back up on the roof, she and Andrew headed to where Reese waited with the chopper.

She frowned when she noticed Reese had shut the machine down. He stood outside the helicopter, his expression grim as he stared at the aircraft.

"What's wrong?" Samantha asked.

"Ice on the blades. It's amazing we made it here in one piece. We'll have to de-ice before we can head back to the Lifeline hangar."

Reese's thigh muscles quivered with the effort of keeping himself upright as the bones in his legs seemingly disintegrated into dust. His face felt frozen but he couldn't relax. He refused to let the rest of the crew know how badly this had shaken him.

They'd almost crashed.

In fact, he had no clue why they hadn't.

Red dots swam before his eyes until he feared he'd end up much like the unconscious patient they'd unloaded a few minutes ago. He didn't want to believe what he'd seen, but the vision of the ice-covered blades was indelibly etched in his brain.

He'd noticed the slightest change in the stick as they'd landed. He wanted to claim instinct had forced him out to double check the chopper but in truth the action had been little more than a whim.

Cripes, five minutes longer and they certainly would have crashed. Or at the very least been forced into a hard landing.

Was this how Valerie had felt in those moments right before the crash? And Greg? Had his best friend noticed the slight hesitation of the stick mid-flight or had the blades just stopped? Did he really want to know what horrible thoughts had gone through his fiancée's and best friend's minds before they'd died?

The frankly curious gazes of Samantha and Andrew, watching as he de-iced the chopper, was all that kept him from sinking to his knees.

"Reese, do you need help?"

Samantha's lyrical, sweet voice helped strengthen his resolve not to show his weakness. *Dr Kearn to you, dummy*, he chided himself. The lady was smart, cool under pressure, and she deserved his respect, not his overly familiar thoughts. He didn't turn around but sensed rather than heard her come up behind him. A light evergreen scent teased his nostrils, kicking his pulse into high gear. The taste of metallic fear faded, quickly replaced by the slightest stirring of lust.

"No, thanks. I'll be finished in a few minutes." His voice sounded wooden to his ears, but hopefully Samantha wouldn't notice.

Dr Kearn. Get it through your cement skull, she's Dr Kearn.

"This is a first, being grounded to de-ice," she admitted softly, stepping into the line of his peripheral vision. "I guess it's better to be safe than sorry."

No, it was better to be safe than *dead*. The living were the only ones who were sorry. Reese mentally drew himself back on track. No sense in scaring the daylights out of the rest of the crew. Better that he keep his dark thoughts to himself.

"There, I'm finished." He verified the chemicals had performed their magic and pronounced the helicopter back in flying form. "I'll put this stuff away, then we can board."

"Reese?"

Bracing himself, he slowly turned to face her. For a moment he couldn't speak. She was so beautiful, no matter how hard she tried not to be. She'd caught his eye the very first day, her glorious red hair pulled back into a no-nonsense braid and her creamy complexion free of makeup. She appeared oblivious to the male attention she drew from the other residents and crew. Several other pilots had commented about her, wondering about her availability, but Reese noticed she never made a flirtatious gesture or remark. Almost as if she made it a point to never cross the line of polite friendliness. The "off-limits" signs couldn't have been any clearer.

Which was fine with him. He was happy enough to admire her from afar. She'd only be part of Lifeline for another few months, then she'd graduate and become a full-fledged physician, making room for the next batch of newbies.

"Yes?"

"With the ice on the blades, how close were we to crashing?"

He hesitated, about to gloss the whole thing over, then decided lying wasn't fair, not when her life had been as much on the line as his. "Too close."

"I see." Her narrow eyebrows drew together to form a solemn line. "Thanks for telling me."

He nearly groaned. Dammit, why couldn't she be a bitch and yell at him or something? He deserved that much. He was the captain. He'd almost gotten her killed.

"Get your gear." His brusque response dimmed the sparkle in her eyes but he told himself it was for the best. Theirs was a professional relationship, nothing more. He quickly stashed the supplies back in the chopper and then pulled the bird out of the hangar. Within moments, they were airborne once again.

The return ride was less than five minutes, but there was an obvious lack of chatter amongst the crew as he set the helicopter on the ground. He gave Samantha and Andrew the signal to disembark, then shut down the engine.

Reese took a few extra moments to go through the basic post-flight checklist, then headed into the Lifeline lounge. Andrew and Samantha were standing there, along with some sort of delivery man holding an enormous flower.

"Dr Samantha Kearn?" the guy was asking, as he glanced at his clipboard. When she nodded, he continued, "Flower delivery for you, ma'am. Please, sign here."

He thrust his clipboard at her and she signed the form, a careful blankness in her normally expressive gray eyes. Reese frowned. What the hell was this? Most women were thrilled with surprise gifts, but Samantha looked green, as if she might throw up.

"Wow, Dr Kearn, someone loves you," Andrew teased. "Who are they from? Hey, there isn't a card."

The tiny hairs on the back of Reese's neck lifted in alarm. The delivery man thrust the flower at her, but Samantha quickly pulled away her hands and stumbled backward out of his reach, then gestured at the table. "No, ah, set it there, please."

There was something wrong with this picture. Reese recognized pure fright when he saw it. Hell, Samantha looked as awful as he'd felt when he'd seen the ice coating the blades.

"Andrew, did you file the flight paperwork yet?" he spoke up quickly.

The paramedic shot him a guilty look. "No, but I will."

"Good. I have my report here, too. Let's get these finished."

Andrew took the not too subtle hint and obediently left the lounge. Reese followed more slowly. Outside the doorway, though, he hesitated then turned to walk back inside, just in time to see Samantha gingerly pick up the flower, still encased in its plastic wrap, and hurtle it into the metal trash can in the corner. A loud crash reverberated through the room.

Definitely, something wrong.

"Who sent it?" Reese asked softly. He wasn't just being nosy, he could feel Samantha's tension all the way across the room. A part of him wanted to protect her from whoever was bothering her.

Samantha spun around to face him, swallowed hard, then squared her shoulders and bravely met his gaze. "There wasn't a card."

"Still, you know who sent it, don't you?"

She remained stubbornly silent but the guilty flash and abrupt lowering of her eyes was answer enough.

CHAPTER TWO

SAM froze, caught by the imploring gaze of Reese's dark eyes. She knew he was waiting for her to tell what she knew, but she didn't want to admit her past failures out loud, and especially not to the handsome chopper pilot.

During the flight, she'd felt connected to Reese, as if their minds were completely in sync, each instinctively working together to bring Jamie safely to Trinity. He'd helped her as much as Andrew had, maybe more. She knew Reese deserved part of the credit for making her first solo flight a resounding success.

But when she'd returned to the hangar and found the lily, her brief euphoria had faded, replaced by a sick clenching in her gut. Denis Markowicz, her controlling ex-husband, had found her again. Once she'd loved lilies, until Denis had showered her with them over and over again. Now the very scent of a lily made her ill.

They'd been divorced for over a year. Why did he persist in seeking ways to make her life miserable?

Because he can, she silently admitted. *Because I let him, by overreacting to his childish gestures.* In a few months she'd graduate and take her emergency medicine boards to become a physician. How was it that the minute Denis pulled one of his stunts she felt helplessly trapped in his manipulations?

Self-doubt seeped through her mind. Maybe Denis was right. Maybe she'd never make it alone.

As quickly as the thought came, she shoved it away. She was strong. She could do this.

"You know who sent it, don't you?"

Since Reese was still looking at her expectantly, she forced herself to answer. "No, I don't." She kept her expression carefully blank, hoping Reese wouldn't notice her hands were shaking.

"Sure you do. It's okay, I understand."

His matter-of-fact statement caught her off guard. She fought the urge to confess. Usually, she could keep one step ahead of prying questions. She'd certainly had more than enough practice at hiding the truth.

She strove to sound casual. "Doesn't matter. Past history." Holding his gaze wasn't easy. Nearly six feet tall and broad-shouldered, Reese was the strong, silent type. He didn't talk about himself much but he had a knack for drawing out confidences from others.

Heck, one look from his melt-your-heart chocolate-brown eyes and she'd nearly blabbed the truth.

For a long moment, he simply waited. His intent expression spoke volumes, basically telling her he knew she was lying and was debating whether or not to call her on it. Finally, he nodded.

"I'm here for you, if you need anything. You can always call me."

"Sure thing." She released her breath in a soundless sigh. Not that she planned to seek him out, but if she did choose to confide in him, what would his reaction be? Would Reese look down on her for being divorced, or would he understand her desperation to be free from her husband's overly controlling nature? As a woman in a male-dominated profession, she knew only too well how the male species stuck together.

Reese turned away, then glanced back over his shoulder. "Dr Kearn?"

His formal address almost made her wince. So much for feeling as if they were true partners in flight. He didn't use titles when he spoke with any of the others, so it couldn't be by accident that he'd singled her out. "Yes?"

"If you really don't want any more deliveries, let Security know. We take our safety very seriously around here."

Samantha stared after his retreating figure. Did he think she would do anything to harm the crew?

Denis wanted to control her, to convince her to come back to him, not to physically hurt her. Reese didn't have to act as if she was a total safety risk.

Some of her anger evaporated, though, because she knew Reese only cared about keeping them safe. And she hadn't told Reese the truth, so how could he know Denis's intent? Besides, the way Denis had found her at Lifeline was creepy. She hadn't heard from him in two months, so why now? Should she make plans to move out of her new apartment? Quit her Lifeline rotation? She could just imagine what Dr Ben Harris, her boss and the medical director of Trinity's Emergency Department, would think about that.

Endless questions rattled in her brain like a box of uncooked noodles. Now that Denis had found her, he wasn't likely to just simply leave her alone. Maybe she should call the police, tell them about the lily? After the divorce she'd taken out a restraining order against Denis, for all the good it did. She crossed the room toward the phone, then stopped.

There wasn't a card, which meant they wouldn't be able to prove Denis had sent the flower. Oh, they'd investigate the flower shop where the delivery had originated, but she'd been down that road before. No doubt the transaction had been made with cash and if Denis had run true to form, he'd found someone else to do his dirty work, ensuring there would be no tracing the lily to him.

The one thing Denis excelled at was covering his tracks.

Samantha gave herself a mental shake. Better to stop dwelling on Denis the Menace. Agonizing over his next move played right into his psycho scheme. She detested his ability to intrude on her thoughts.

Abruptly she straightened and squared her shoulders. What was she worried about? She was a free and independent woman, not the naïve person who'd married too young. It was about time Denis realized the truth.

She was determined to remain immune to his mind games.

Despite her determination to forget her past, the heavy, cloying scent of the lily seemed to follow her as she restocked the supplies they'd used from the flight bag. She was glad to be alone, away from Reese's all too knowing brown eyes. What she wouldn't give for a call now. Something to occupy her mind would be heavenly.

"Hungry?" Reese asked from the doorway of the supply room.

She snapped her head around. Already, her muscles were tighter than a coiled spring. She let her breath out in a soundless sigh. "Uh, sure. Give me a few minutes."

Reese waited patiently for her to finish. His silent presence was overwhelmingly close and her fingers turned clumsy, nearly dropping a small stack of catheters on the floor.

She managed to get them packed into the flight bag, then double-checked to make sure she had everything. "I'll put this away and meet you in the lounge."

"I'll take it for you." He easily slid the bag from her grasp.

Logic told her Reese was simply being polite, but his take-charge manner rubbed her up the wrong way. Plus, she couldn't help but wonder if he didn't trust her near the helicopter. She'd noticed over the past few weeks how Reese watched Mitch the mechanic like a hawk while he worked on it. The other crew members teased Reese about it, although he didn't seem to care. And hadn't his reaction to the iced blades been a little strange? Surely, as a pilot, he'd been forced to de-ice choppers before?

Of course, the danger had been very real. He'd admitted as much when she'd asked him point-blank.

Normally she didn't think about the danger of flying any more than ambulance drivers probably considered the threat of a potential crash while they raced to an accident scene. The helicopter was just one means of transport, one she happened to prefer. And Lifeline had an excellent twenty-year crash-free history.

She was just being paranoid. Reese took his responsibilities seriously. So seriously, she wondered about him sometimes. During these past few weeks she couldn't remember ever hearing him laugh out loud. But Reese's somber attitude wasn't her concern. She couldn't afford to worry about him. Her goal was to graduate and move on with her own life, in that order.

Andrew joined her in the lounge. A few minutes later, Reese strode in.

"What are you hungry for? Take-out pizza or the deli across the street?" Reese wanted to know.

Samantha almost requested pizza until she realized it was only to avoid going outside because she feared seeing Denis. *Don't do this*, she warned herself. *Don't let him force you into hiding from life. This is all a part of his need for control.*

"The deli." She quickly spoke up before she could change her mind.

Andrew grinned and rubbed his hands together. "Yeah, I'm in the mood for a Reuben sandwich."

They grabbed their thick quilted Lifeline jackets as the frigid Wisconsin winter wind was sharp enough to etch steel. Reese gestured for them to precede him out the door. Sam kept her gaze forward as they crossed the street, refusing to search for signs of Denis following her.

The deli was packed with people, even on such a cold day. They were close enough that if a call came in, they'd still be able to get into the air within the designated five-minute time frame. They stood in line and placed their order, then waited another few minutes until their food was ready. Samantha only hoped she'd have time to finish her turkey before the next call came in.

While the noisy deli was hardly an intimate atmosphere, she was keenly aware of the slightest brush of Reese's knee against hers as the three of them sat around a small table. When his knee stayed warmly against hers, she waited for him to move. When he didn't, she subtly shifted away. Concentrating on her food, she knew she was being ridiculous. No doubt Reese hadn't even noticed the innocent touch.

"I still can't believe you inserted a chest tube in flight," Andrew gushed around a mouthful of his corned beef sandwich. "That was totally awesome."

Reese raised a brow. "Is a chest tube such an unusual procedure?"

Sam shrugged. "Not really. It's pretty commonplace in the emergency department." Andrew's praise made her uncomfortable. She'd been worried during the procedure, but Reese's calm voice had helped keep her fingers steady.

"I've been at Lifeline for three years and I haven't seen it done until today," Andrew stubbornly persisted.

Sam ate her turkey, but she could feel Reese's intent gaze on her, as he seemed to silently agree with Andrew's assessment.

At least her medical skills were something to be proud of, not like her personal life. There, she was a complete failure.

The morose thought caused her appetite to evaporate. She crumpled her napkin and tossed it on her half-eaten food. "I'm finished, so I'm heading back."

Before she could stand, Reese's hand clasped her arm. She caught her breath at his touch. His fingers were warm, holding her securely but nowhere near hard enough to bruise. "Wait. Don't go alone."

The urge to pull away and stomp out of there was strong. Instinctively, she bristled. Who was he to tell her what to do?

"I'm fine. Really." She flashed them both a reassuring smile.

"Please?"

His quiet plea stopped her from leaving as nothing else would have. Denis had never asked, he'd demanded. She knew not every man was like her ex, but somehow her first reaction was to lash out as if they were.

"I guess I can wait." She settled back into her seat.

"Thank you." Reese stared at her for a moment, then slowly drew his hand from her arm.

She almost stroked the spot where he'd touched her, amazed at the strange, tingling sensation left by his warm grip. Normally her skin crawled when a man touched her. What had changed? Why didn't she have the same reaction with Reese Jarvis?

She couldn't come up with a good answer as the

guys finished their meal in record time, no doubt virtually inhaling their food on her behalf, just so she wouldn't have to wait.

Guilt returned full force. "Don't rush. It's not as if we have calls waiting," she urged them.

"We're not rushing, are we?" Reese asked Andrew, after swallowing his last bit of food.

"Nope. I always eat fast. Drives my wife nuts," Andrew cheerfully replied.

She gave up as they quickly rolled their wrappers into a ball and stood to leave.

Outside, Reese and Andrew fell into step on either side of her as they walked back to the Lifeline hangar. Sam was struck by how hyperaware she was of Reese on her right, while Andrew could have been nonexistent on her left. The faintest whiff of Reese's spicy aftershave enticed her to move closer.

What was wrong with her? Reese certainly seemed like a nice guy but, heaven knew, she'd been wrong before. She didn't have time for this weird attraction. Not when she needed all her energy to focus on finishing her residency and getting her personal life on track.

She would follow Reese's example and keep a professional distance between them. Which shouldn't be too difficult, especially since during their flight time Reese sat in the cockpit.

If she could only get his husky voice out of her head, she'd be fine.

Reese stared at the weather radar screen without seeing a single cloud. Even the icy blades were a distant memory. The strange flower delivery Samantha had received nagged at him, wreaking havoc with his concentration.

Surely it was just the idea she might be in trouble, rather than the woman herself that bothered him?

"Reese?"

He glanced up, startled to find the woman occupying his thoughts standing in front of him. Samantha—or rather Dr Kearn—looked incredibly tiny in the figure-hugging flight suit. Too small to hold her own against some creep bugging her with a stupid gift.

"I want you to know, I called Security."

He was surprised at her frank admission. The way she'd refused to tell him the truth earlier had him betting she would have continued to deny anything was wrong. A surge of anger about the situation caught him off guard. Who in the hell had sent the thing to her, anyway? And why didn't she just tell the creep to shove off? "Good. I'm glad."

"So there's no need to worry about a security breach." Samantha's gaze bored into his for a moment, then she gestured to the screen. "How much longer before the snow clears?"

"Not sure. Another hour at least." Reese frowned when she turned to leave. "Wait a minute, I wasn't implying you had caused a breach in security."

"Weren't you?" Her cool tone flayed him. She spun on her heel and stalked away.

Reese stared after her, then dropped his head into his hand. Man, he'd really botched that one. He'd never intended to hurt her, but maybe it was better she stay ticked at him. Her slender arm had felt far too good beneath his hand. Listening to her husky voice through the headset in flight was bad enough. Every word she spoke made him think of soft down blankets and endless winter nights. Being so close to her was tempting. He never should have touched her.

He'd watched many like her come and go. Senior emergency medicine residents did their required rotations, then left to graduate as full-fledged physicians. The only full-time doctor on staff was Dr Jared O'Connor, and he was a pediatric specialist as well as the medical director of the program.

Seeing the residents come and go had never bothered him before, especially the women. He wasn't in the market for a relationship. Ever. The pain of losing someone you loved was too devastating. Didn't he see the same theme over and over again with every injured or sick person they transported? Every patient had someone who mourned the potential loss of wife, father, sister or child. He'd been down that road before and had no intention of repeating the experience.

More than enough reason to remind himself the beautiful Dr Kearn was off-limits.

A call came in, requesting a response to a crash scene. Samantha materialized in the doorway before he'd finished reading the entire message on his pager.

"Ready to go?"

"I don't think so." Reese gestured to the radar screen. "The snow is getting thick and heavy. The higher the altitude, the more likely the snow will be freezing rain. Temperatures are hovering around freezing. Dangerous flying weather."

Her frown was perplexed. "But we've flown in snow before."

Reese hesitated for a moment, then shrugged. He knew there were pilots who pushed the line of safe flying, but he wasn't one of them. Snow in and of itself didn't justify red flying conditions, but freezing rain did, and the temperature was too fickle right now to make the distinction. Swallowing his own disappointment, he picked up the phone to call the paramedic base. "Base, we're in yellow flying conditions that are leaning toward red. I don't think we should respond to this call."

"Roger, we'll notify the paramedic unit closest to the scene."

Samantha stared at him for a long minute and he braced himself for the arguments he could practically see dancing in her head. To his surprise, though, she simply turned and left.

Guilt weighted heavy on his heart. There was only an hour left until the end of their twelve-hour shift and Reese reminded himself how keeping the crew safe was his top priority. The crash victims would get the aid they needed. Still, he silently admitted he didn't like turning down anyone in distress. Their purpose was to save lives, but he knew from painful firsthand experience that he couldn't save anyone by putting the crew at risk.

The weather had been similar, thick, wet swirling snow, the night Greg and Valerie had crashed. He had tortured himself for weeks after their deaths, wondering if he could have prevented it. Reese had switched shifts with Greg so he could take his grandmother to her doctor's appointment. Greg had been his friend, but Greg had also been known for being a risky flier. He'd been arrogant, thinking his skills at the stick had far outweighed the threat from the weather.

Had Valerie been willing to go along or had she tried to get Greg to call off the flight? Reese had no way of knowing the truth. He could only comfort himself with the knowledge that Valerie had loved being a flight nurse and had accepted the risks just like the rest of them.

He didn't realize how long he'd been staring morosely at the radar screen until the pilot coming on shift, Nate, strode into the debriefing room. "Hey, Reese. How's the weather?"

"I've seen better." Reese subtly glanced at his watch. Surprise widened his eyes. Where had the last hour gone?

"Are we in the red?"

"Yellow, but I turned down a scene call a while ago." Reese glanced over Nate's shoulder. "When the rest of the crew arrives, I'll fill you in."

Within five minutes Kate and another senior resident, Dr Zach Wilson, entered the debriefing room. Reese quickly gave them an update on the ice incident and the impact of the weather conditions. Samantha and Andrew briefed them on the transport they'd done earlier that day, including the placement of the chest tube. Kate and Zach were impressed by Samantha's quick thinking.

She flushed and averted her gaze, obviously uncomfortable with the attention. Many of the physicians were a bit on the arrogant side, a fact he readily accepted. He'd always figured you had to be a tad arrogant to work in such a stressful job and, truthfully, pilots were similar in many ways. Samantha was different and he couldn't help but wonder if the mystery guy who'd sent the flower was part of the reason she didn't like being the center of attention.

Reese purposefully waited until she and Andrew left the debriefing room before adding another portion of his report, one he preferred to give out of Dr Kearn's earshot.

"Security has been instructed not to accept any gifts of any nature for Dr Kearn," he confided.

"Gifts?" Kate's eyes widened. "Why ever not? I'd love for someone to send me gifts."

Reese frowned. "Maybe, but I don't think Dr Kearn's gift was a token of appreciation. The details aren't our business."

"They are, if there's a threat involved," Nate argued.

"A flower isn't exactly a threat." Reese lifted a hand to halt another argument. "I'll let Jared know, although I'm certain Dr Kearn will take care of that, too. Still, for now, just make a notation in the book that no deliveries are to be accepted on behalf of Dr Kearn."

Nate muttered under his breath, but reluctantly agreed. Reese grabbed his coat and left the hangar.

Being a weekend, there weren't many cars in the parking lot, especially at seven-thirty in the evening. Darkness had fallen, but the fresh white snow covering the ground glittered like shards of glass in the moonlight. Reese blinked through the swirling snowflakes, noticing how the wheels of a large dark-colored Oldsmobile spun uselessly in the snow. Since Andrew drove a minivan, he figured Samantha was the driver.

"Hey!" He waved to get Samantha's attention and hastened over to tap on her window. "I have a truck. Why don't you let me drive you home?"

She rolled down the window. "No, thanks, I'm fine."

"Come on, the streets are bound to be slippery and I have four-wheel drive. No reason to have two cars on the road."

"Look, Reese, I don't need your help. Thanks anyway." Even as she spoke, she stomped hard on the accelerator and the rear wheels caught enough pavement that her ancient Oldsmobile lurched forward.

Reese stood in the snow, staring after her as she drove off.

CHAPTER THREE

SAMANTHA rested her forehead on the top of the steering wheel and uttered a low groan. Things had happened so fast, she didn't even remember sliding into the ditch. Stupid bunny just had to run into the middle of the road. She'd swerved to avoid hitting it and had ended up with her rear tires stuck in the ditch for her efforts.

Yep. Reese had been right. The roads were slick.

She sighed, lifted her head and tried rocking her car out of the ditch again. No dice. She was good and stuck.

No use dwelling on the situation. At least she wasn't too far from the Oak Terrace apartment building where she lived. The walk would do her good. The only hassle would be getting to work in the morning without a car.

She opened her door and watched a big black truck pull alongside her. For a moment her heart raced with fear, until she recognized Reese's concerned face peering at her through his open passenger window.

"Are you all right?"

"Just dandy." Sam braced herself for the "I told you so" he was bound to say.

"Will you allow me to give you a ride home? Or would you rather I try to push your car out?"

Surprised, she stared at him. He was giving her a

choice? Without trying to tell her how idiotic she was to drive into the ditch in the first place? How amazing.

"I have to work early in the morning, so I'd really like to get my car out, if you don't mind."

He nodded, seemingly not surprised by her request. "I don't mind. I'll park up ahead, then push you out."

Sam was grateful he didn't give her a lecture, or rub in how foolish she was. She had a feeling Reese wouldn't have swerved for a bunny, or if he had, his truck had four-wheel drive so he wouldn't have ended up in the ditch. True to his word, he trudged past her open driver's side window to the back of her car, checking where her wheels had slid off the road.

"Do you know how to rock the car?" he wanted to know.

"Yes."

"Good. Start rocking and I'll give you a push." His voice was muffled, and in her rearview mirror she saw he was braced along the bumper behind the passenger side rear wheel.

"Here goes," she muttered. She hit the gas intermittently, setting up a rocking motion. Once. Twice. Three times. Four.

Without warning, her tire caught hold and her car shot up the embankment onto the road. She quickly hit the brakes.

Reese scrambled up after her, then jumped into the passenger seat of her car. The Olds was almost eighteen years old and didn't have anything resembling automatic locks.

She cranked up the heat for his benefit, then turned

to him, flashing a warm smile. "Thanks, Reese. I really appreciate your help."

"You're welcome. For a minute there I thought you were planning to walk home. Do you live far from here?"

"No. About a mile or two down the road in the Oak Terrace Apartments."

"Really?" His eyebrows shot up in surprise. "Me, too."

Reese lived in the same complex? She'd never seen him around, but then again she'd only lived there for a couple of months. "Which building?"

"The South building."

"Oh, I live in the North building." Which probably explained why she hadn't seen him yet. The news Reese lived so close didn't alarm her. Instead, a flicker of excitement danced along her nerves. Now that she knew he lived so close, she'd drive herself crazy watching for him.

An awkward silence fell between them. He didn't make an effort to get out of her car and Sam wasn't sure what she should do. She didn't feel right kicking him out of her car after he had gone to the trouble of pushing her out of the ditch. But what on earth was he waiting for?

"Do you mind if I ask you a personal question?"

Her gut clenched in warning. "Uh, no, I guess not."

His hair was damp from the melting snow and he slanted her a sideways glance. "Are you married?"

"No!" Cheeks burning with mortification, she couldn't believe he'd thought she was married.

Samantha knew she didn't owe him an explanation, but found herself telling him anyway. "I'm divorced."

The relief in his expression nearly made her smile. Then his brows pulled together in a dark frown. "Is your ex the one who sent the flower?"

How had he guessed? Reluctantly, she nodded. "He's persistent."

"What's his name?"

"Denis Markowicz."

"How long have you been divorced?"

"A year."

"More than persistent, then."

She couldn't argue, but Denis was the last person she wanted to talk about. He was the past, her goal was to focus on the future. The hour was getting late, and she really did have to work in the morning. "Well, thanks again. Did you want me to drive you home?"

"Huh?" Reese glanced around as if he'd forgotten he was still sitting in her car. "Oh, no. But wait for me and I'll follow you."

Before she could respond one way or the other, he opened the door and climbed from the car.

Sam swallowed a protest, watching as he hunched his shoulders against the cold wind and headed for his truck. He didn't need to follow her home, but since they were going the same way, there wasn't any point in arguing.

Besides, her pulse still hadn't settled back to normal after he'd asked if she was married. Had he simply been fishing for information on who'd sent the lily? Or had he wanted to know her marital status for personal reasons?

When he flashed his lights, she pulled out into the nonexistent traffic ahead of him. Reese's truck lights were reassuringly bright behind her.

Despite her vow to concentrate on her career, forgetting the mistakes in her past, Sam found herself secretly hoping Reese had asked about her marital status for personal reasons.

The ride home was a short one. She pulled into an empty parking space in front of her North building, fully expecting Reese to continue on. But he surprised her by parking his truck beside her car.

She climbed from the Olds, glancing over as he did the same. "What are you doing?"

"I thought I'd walk you in." Reese slammed his truck door behind him.

"There's no reason to walk me in," she protested.

"Hey, humor me, will you?" Reese fell into step beside her. "What's the harm?"

Sam shrugged, unable to think of a reason not to. He was certainly going out of his way to be nice. Too bad she wasn't in the market for a man. She shot him a quick look as they headed up the sidewalk. Did he think she was? In the market for a man?

Her boots slid in the slippery snow and he quickly cupped a hand under her elbow. "Easy, don't fall."

She wanted to point out she was already falling, the ground seemingly disappearing from beneath her feet. Every time Reese touched her, she was free-falling into new territory. Having Reese's undivided attention was a completely disarming experience. One that shifted her off balance.

She used her key to access the building. Once inside, Reese paused in front of the elevator. "Which floor?"

"Ground level." She brushed past him to unlock the second door. One of the reasons she liked this apartment building was because of the fairly decent security.

"This way." She turned left and headed down the hall to her apartment. Outside the door, she turned and forced a smile. "This is it. Thanks for walking me in."

"No problem."

When he didn't immediately leave, she raised a brow. Now what? "Are you planning to follow me inside?"

"Just enough to make sure there are no surprises." Reese's expression never changed, but she thought his eyes darkened.

"I'm sure he didn't deliver a lily here." She suppressed a sigh and unlocked her door. She opened it with one hand, finding and switching on the lights with the other. A quick sweeping glance confirmed there was nothing out of order.

"See? Everything's fine." She stepped back against the door, gesturing for him to look for himself.

Reese nodded again and stepped closer, craning his neck to see the inside of her apartment. She caught another whiff of his spicy aftershave and shrank back against the door to stop from throwing herself into his arms. Dear heaven, what was wrong with her? Reese was just being nice. Was she so unused to nice behavior from a man that she couldn't recognize it for what it was?

"Thanks again, Reese. See you tomorrow." She injected cheerfulness into her tone to hide her confusion. Taking several side steps, she eased along the door, heading into her apartment. Reese didn't have to do anything more than stand there and look at her to crumble her instinctive resistance toward the male species.

His gaze met hers and time hung suspended between them. He was very close, his eyes darkly intent. For a moment she wondered if he might lean forward and kiss her. Her lips parted in anticipation. If he did, would she be brave enough to kiss him back?

"Goodnight, Samantha." His voice was low, husky, drawing out the syllables of her name in a rumbling tone. Dazed and breathless, she realized he'd used her full name. Samantha. No more Dr Kearn, she was Samantha now. "See you tomorrow."

Speechless, she could only stare after him as he turned and ambled away. Realizing she was standing with the door wide open, staring down an empty hallway, she quickly closed and locked it, then leaned against the wood, her head tilted back against the door, her heart beating rapidly in her chest.

Reese wasn't a part of her master plan, but somehow she suspected he wasn't going to be easy to ignore.

And the thought brought a thrill of anticipation she hadn't experienced in years.

* * *

The snow was falling in thick, swirling flakes as Reese headed outside toward his truck. Reese lifted his face, the snow a welcome coolness against his flushed skin.

Stripping down to cool off the rest of his libido wasn't an option, although he was sorely tempted. Didn't the Swedish believe in bathing their entire body in snow? At the moment he was so hot he suspected he'd melt the snow into a steaming puddle in two seconds flat.

Damn, he needed to get a grip. He'd called her Samantha. He liked her name, but that wasn't the point. What had happened to Dr Kearn? She was supposed to stay Dr Kearn. How could he keep her out of his head now that he'd called her Samantha?

Reese drove around Samantha's building to his assigned parking space. He shut off the engine and got out of the truck then locked the doors. Plowing through the snow, he didn't notice the sharp wind in his face. Inside the building, he headed to his apartment.

The layout was an exact replica of Samantha's, only he was on the second floor. As he threw his keys on the table, he wondered how she was doing. After the day she'd had, she deserved to relax in a tub full of sudsy water.

Don't go there. Imagining Samantha, her glorious red hair piled haphazardly on top of her head, her body wearing nothing but bubbles, really thin, transparent bubbles, was not going to help him relax.

What in Hades was wrong with him?

She'd gotten to him, although she clearly hadn't

tried to involve him. No, in fact, he was rather ticked about how he'd had to drag information from her. He hadn't imagined the instant flare of panic in her eyes when he'd pulled up beside her car when she'd been stuck in the ditch.

So Samantha liked her privacy. Big deal. Did he really blame her? He understood how she felt. He hadn't announced his miserable past for everyone at Lifeline to lament over.

Valerie. With a guilty start, Reese realized he hadn't really thought about his late fiancée at all since earlier that day. And even then, only because the ice on his blades had reminded him of the crash. For a moment he tried to imagine Valerie's tanned features, her easy smile, but instead Samantha emerged from the mist of his memory. Samantha's creamy skin, her red hair pulled into that no-nonsense braid, her tentative smile.

The shadow of fear in her eyes.

Today was the anniversary of Valerie's and Greg's deaths. Yet somehow being with Samantha had managed to obliterate his sadness and regret. There wasn't anything he could do to help Valerie now, but he could help Samantha feel safe during the remaining months of her Lifeline rotation.

At least until she graduated from her residency and moved on.

CHAPTER FOUR

REESE left his apartment to head to work early, but he was disappointed to note Samantha's ancient vehicle was already missing from her parking spot. They should carpool to work, since they lived so close.

He winced and mentally thumped himself in the head at the inane thought. Who was he trying to kid? He didn't give a hoot about saving fuel, it wasn't as if the Oak Terrace apartment complex was far from Lifeline. No, what he really wanted was an excuse to spend more time with Samantha.

Stupid idea, dreaming up ways to spend more time with her. They were scheduled to fly together often enough as it was. Sleep had been a long time in coming last night, thanks to his overactive imagination. He'd woken hard and aching for something he couldn't have.

Inside the Lifeline hangar, he found Samantha standing in the debriefing room. He could have used a crowbar to pry his tongue from the roof of his mouth when he saw her. Her fresh, clean beauty literally took his breath away. There was nothing spectacular about the regulation navy blue flight suit she wore, but she'd left the zipper open a few inches, revealing the white turtleneck beneath. The material almost entirely covered her skin, but for some reason on her the white turtleneck sweater was incredibly sexy.

"Good morning."

"Hello, Reese." Her brief smile was gone before he had a chance to fully appreciate it. He tried to think of something to say that might bring it back.

Mentally, he gave a snort. Enough already. He and Samantha were flight partners, nothing more. Time to get back on friendship footing. "So how's the weather?" he asked.

"Clear skies. We're good to go," Nate piped up from his seat beside the radar screen.

"Great. Then we don't need to refuse any calls," Samantha replied.

Reese raised a brow at her irritable tone. "I don't like refusing calls either, you know."

"I know. But there's nothing worse than feeling helpless. At least we know today if something comes in, we can respond." She glanced at Nate. "Are there any transfers waiting in the wings?"

"Nope." Nate shook his head.

Reese took off his jacket and carried it to the small pilots' room adjacent to the debriefing area. He mulled over Samantha's words as he hung up his jacket behind the door. None of them liked being grounded, but Samantha had mentioned helplessness. A leftover emotion from her marriage? She hadn't confided the details of her breakup and now he wanted to know. Had her ex-husband made her feel helpless? Had he used his strength against her?

Anger seethed at the very thought, but he reined himself in with an effort. His imagination was working overtime again. Just because Samantha hated feeling helpless, that didn't mean there was physical abuse in her past.

Besides, a guy who was abusive probably wouldn't bother sending flowers. Calmer now, he laughed at himself for jumping to conclusions. So what was the deal with the lily?

Shaking his head at his insatiable curiosity, Reese made his way back into the debriefing area. His pager went off simultaneously with Samantha's.

"'Motor vehicle crash on the interstate, one adult victim in critical condition'," he read aloud. He glanced at Samantha. "Where's Andrew? Are you ready to go?"

"He's getting coffee, but it can wait. We're ready."

Reese walked behind Samantha, her faint evergreen scent teasing his nostrils. What did she do, shower with a Christmas tree every morning? He wanted to scrub the image of sharing a shower with her, minus the Christmas tree, from his mind.

"Andrew, come on," Samantha called as they passed the lounge. With a frown the young paramedic set his freshly poured coffee aside and followed them out to the hangar.

All three of them grabbed helmets, then Reese headed for the chopper while Samantha and Andrew double-checked the flight bag of medical supplies. First Reese opened the hangar door then, using the triangular rolling base, he pushed the lightweight helicopter outside into the frigid air.

Samantha and Andrew quickly followed, jumping

into the helicopter through the side doors with the flight bag in tow.

Reese climbed into the cockpit and quickly plugged in his headset so he wouldn't miss one minute of listening to Samantha's sweet voice.

Man, he had it bad.

With a resigned shake of his head, he started the engine. The crash scene wasn't far, just to the south about twenty miles. He communicated with the base, then told the rest of the crew to prepare for takeoff.

Samantha and Andrew were quiet in the back and he wondered what they were thinking. Maybe Andrew was still half-asleep, since he hadn't gotten his daily dose of caffeine. Reese stared down at the ribbon of highway below, taking note of the glaring sunlight from the east. He'd need to land in such a way as to avoid having the full force of the sun in his eyes on takeoff.

The mangled cars and rescue vehicles at the scene of the crash were visible from his vantage point in the air. Cueing his mike, he alerted Samantha and Andrew.

"ETA four minutes."

"Roger. We can see the crash site." Samantha's lyrical voice caused his gut to tighten with awareness. He forced himself to concentrate on power lines and choosing the best place to land.

There was a large grassy field on the west side of the highway, where most of the debris from the crash was scattered. From the looks of things, the victims were in the field as well. He decided there was enough room for him to land in the empty portion of the field, close but not too close to the scene.

He set down the chopper, then flipped the switch, dropping the rotation of the blades to their lowest setting.

"You're clear to go," he told them.

Through his window, Reese watched Andrew and Samantha exit the helicopter. He held his breath when they opened the back hatch and pulled out the gurney, the tail of the chopper being the most dangerous. In moments he saw them running alongside the gurney as they wheeled it over to the crash site.

Sitting in the cockpit while the crew attended to the victims was the hardest part of his job. The pilot's job was to stay with the bird, he understood the rules. You never knew if there was some whacko that would try to jump into an empty helicopter if he left it unattended. Still, understanding the rules didn't mean he had to like them.

The sun glinted brightly on the fiery-red hue of Samantha's hair. She and Andrew knelt beside a female victim and Reese noticed a paramedic was holding back a man who appeared to be trying to get to the woman's side.

Her boyfriend? Husband? The frank anguish on the man's features reminded him of the day he'd received the phone call about Valerie and Greg's crash. The pain of losing someone you loved was indescribable.

Samantha and Andrew had already placed the victim on the gurney and seemed to be getting ready to bring her to the helicopter. Reese was glad. Their actions meant the woman was still alive, still had a chance at survival. He tapped his foot impatiently as he waited for them to approach.

The paramedic still held on to the guy who Reese could only assume had been in the crash with the woman. Samantha and Andrew had almost reached the helicopter when the guy broke loose from the paramedic's hold.

With a muttered curse Reese shut down the engines as the guy ran straight for the gurney. He yanked off his helmet, pushed open the door and jumped to the ground. He dashed toward Samantha and Andrew.

"Look out," he shouted.

The distraught man grabbed at the woman on the gurney, nearly knocking Samantha to the ground with his force. "Becky!" the guy cried. "Oh, God, Becky!"

Reese grabbed the guy's arm before he could dislodge any of the lifesaving medical equipment Samantha may have connected to the patient. "Hey, buddy, you're not helping us here. She needs medical attention. We need to get her to the hospital as soon as possible."

"I want to come with you." The guy was strong, and Reese had to dig his boot heels into the earth to prevent himself from being tossed aside.

"You can't come along," Samantha said, regret shadowing her eyes as she held on to the gurney. "I'm sorry, but I promise we'll take good care of her."

"I'm coming, dammit!" The guy yanked hard against the hold Reese had on him. "Becky, don't worry, hon. I'm coming with you."

Reese wrestled the guy's grip off the gurney, then met Samantha's gaze over his head. "Get her into the helicopter, quick."

Samantha and Andrew ran with the gurney toward the back hatch door. Reese hoped the paramedics were on their way to help him subdue the man or they'd never be able to get off the ground without him trying something stupid like jumping on for a ride.

Luckily, the paramedics saw what was happening and came to the rescue.

"Whoa, Jake, what are you doing?" One of them got in front of the man while the other helped Reese hang on to his arms. "You're not helping Becky, man. She needs to get to the hospital, fast."

The two paramedics worked together to force Jake to the ground. Once he was down, Reese was able to relinquish his hold on him.

"Keep him down until we're gone," he tersely advised.

The paramedics nodded their agreement. The one who'd been holding on to Jake earlier added, "He's not injured that we can see, but we'll probably have to sedate him and transport him to Trinity anyway."

"Good luck." Reese dashed to the helicopter and climbed in.

Samantha and Andrew were already safely inside with their patient. Without wasting time, Reese quickly buckled in, pulled on his helmet and notified the base they were lifting off. He guided the helicopter off the ground, keeping a wary eye on the two paramedics holding down the irrational Jake.

When he had cleared the tops of the trees and the power lines, Reese took a deep breath. For a few minutes there he'd wondered if they'd make it without mishap. He knew just how poor Jake must have felt, watching helplessly as Samantha and Andrew had whisked away the woman he loved. Still, the way Jake had plowed into Samantha ticked him off. Thank God she wasn't hurt.

As he banked around toward Trinity, Reese became aware of problems in back with the patient.

"Andrew, get me two more units of blood. We're losing her pressure." Samantha's voice came through his headset. "Come on, where is she bleeding?"

"Her rhythm is fine," Andrew commented. "I'd think if she was bleeding internally she'd be more tachy."

"Not if she has cardiac tamponade or even a hemothorax," Samantha responded. "My gut tells me it's her heart, but I wish I could listen to her lungs and heart tones."

"Do you need me to find a place to land?" Reese asked, flying and listening to the conversation in the back at the same time. With helmets on and communication through an intercom he understood the limitations of air transport. At least he could get them to Trinity or an alternate hospital quickly.

"No, thanks, Reese. I'm going to place a cardiac needle to relieve the pressure. Just get us to Trinity as fast as you can."

"Roger." Thank heavens this was a short trip. They were only five to seven minutes from their destination, so there wasn't much he could do except climb a few more feet in an effort to use the tailwind to its greatest advantage.

"Holy cow!" Andrew's voice came through loudly. "Look at all that blood!"

"Reese, can you radio the base to request that a cardiothoracic surgeon be on standby?" Samantha asked. "I think this woman's going to need open heart surgery."

"Roger." Reese quickly flipped the switch to get in contact with the base, rattling off Samantha's instructions.

The paramedic base responded to his call and he gauged the time remaining until they reached Trinity Medical Center. "ETA three minutes," he informed them.

"Thank God," Andrew muttered.

"Look, her blood pressure is improving. Keep giving her more blood while I hold the needle steady."

"I will."

Reese listened intently as he approached Trinity's helipad. He radioed the base to inform them he was about to land. Within moments he set the chopper down gently in the center.

"All clear," he informed them.

Samantha didn't waste any time. He watched as she and Andrew unloaded their patient and wheeled her quickly to the waiting elevators.

There was nothing more he could do. Reese sat back in his seat and rubbed a hand over his eyes. This was why he needed to fight his secret desire to spend time alone with Samantha. How would he ever survive another loss like that he'd experienced with Valerie?

Poor Jake. Reese could only hope that Samantha's quick diagnosis had saved Becky's life. But as he waited for Samantha to return, he realized telling himself to keep away from Samantha was the easy part. The hard part would be listening to the logical voice in his head. Because every instinct he possessed screamed at him to grab Samantha and to hang on tight.

Sam stood beside Andrew, reluctant to leave although the cardiothoracic team had taken over, wheeling Becky into the OR, preparing her for an exploration of her heart.

"Hey, she'll be fine." Andrew touched her lightly on the arm. "Come on, we'd better go."

She nodded and followed Andrew back to the elevator, riding up to the rooftop landing pad where Reese waited in the Lifeline chopper.

There hadn't been time to dwell on the incident at the scene while in flight, as her patient's condition had been too critical. But now the entire thing seemed surreal. Never before had she been nearly attacked by a distraught family member at a crash scene. If not for Reese holding the guy back, they wouldn't have gotten out of there in time to get Becky safely transported to Trinity.

Outside, Andrew signaled to Reese, who gestured for them to climb in. Inside the helicopter, Andrew began putting supplies away, cleaning up bloodstains with a bleach wipe.

Sam listened as Reese communicated with the base about takeoff. The trip to Lifeline would be quick, she knew, unless they received another call. Reese's husky voice was calm. He'd even been cool and steady when holding back Jake.

What would it take to ruffle his feathers? Sam wasn't sure she wanted to find out.

Back inside Lifeline's lounge, Andrew made a beeline for the coffee machine. Sam hung back, waiting for Reese, following him into the debriefing room.

"I wanted to thank you for what you did back there." She touched his arm lightly, but the heat of his skin radiating through the long sleeve of his flight suit had her drawing back quickly. "For a minute I thought our buddy Jake was going to grab her and take off."

Reese shook his head. "Yeah, I was worried for a few minutes myself." He looked at her intently and his voice dropped intimately. "I wanted to punch him when he knocked you aside like that."

"I'm fine. He wasn't trying to hurt me."

"I know." Reese scrubbed his hands over his face. "He wanted to ride along. Can you imagine what would have happened if he'd have gotten into the helicopter with us?"

"No, I don't even want to think about it," Sam admitted. "I thought he was going to go off the deep end."

"He still may, if she doesn't make it." Reese's voice was quiet as he sat down, staring at his feet. "I hope she does."

Sam tilted her head, a puzzled frown in her brow.

Reese appeared really troubled by this transport and she sensed there was something more going on in his head. And despite knowing she shouldn't get close, she couldn't help but probe. "Hey," she said softly, "are you all right?"

"Me?" He raised his gaze to hers. "Why wouldn't I be?"

The wounded expression had vanished and Sam wondered if she'd imagined it. "I don't know. You seem sad."

"No. I'm fine." He stared at the satellite monitor as if the screen held the answers to world peace, and she suspected he was avoiding her gaze. Finally he spoke. "There's a storm warning for tomorrow."

"Hmm." Obviously, he was avoiding talking to her. For the first time she realized Reese possessed secrets of his own. Secrets he wasn't willing to share. And strangely enough she couldn't help but wonder exactly what those secrets were.

CHAPTER FIVE

ANDREW popped his head into the debriefing room. "Hey, I gotta head over to Trinity for our post-flight follow-up visits."

As much as she wished for a window to peer into Reese's mind to know what he was thinking, the idea of post-flight visits distracted her. "Could I do them?" Samantha asked. "I'd really like to see how some of our patients are faring."

The paramedic hesitated. "There's no reason you couldn't, except the visits are part of my job, not yours."

Samantha didn't care whose job they were. Turning over the care of her patients was the hardest part of being a flight physician and she often wondered how her patients were doing long after she left them. "I don't mind, honestly. And Kate showed me how to fill out the paperwork during training."

Andrew shrugged and handed over the clipboard. "Go ahead, then, if you want to."

"Thanks." Sam glanced at the list of names. Jamie's was top of the list. There were at least three other patients beside Jamie that needed to be checked on. She glanced at Reese. "Do you want to come along?"

He hesitated, then shook his head. "I think there's some rule against giving pilots confidential medical information unless it's directly related to the flight. Go on. I'll wait here and watch Mitch check over the helicopter."

"I'll be back soon," she promised.

"Just hustle back here if a call comes in," Reese cautioned.

"I will." Sam flashed him a quick smile, then grabbed her bulky Lifeline jacket and headed outside.

The trip to Trinity was short as the Lifeline hangar was strategically located nearby. While she walked, her thoughts dwelled on Reese. She really enjoyed flying with him; he was incredibly easy to work with. Of all the pilots, he was the most in tune with what was going on with the patient during transport.

Had she imagined that hint of sorrow in his eyes? She knew he wasn't married, she'd heard the other female residents and the flight nurses talking about Reese in the early days of her training. He was always polite, but she noticed he didn't flirt with the female staff.

Because he wasn't interested? Last night, when he'd walked her to her apartment door, the heated awareness between them had been a palpable thing. She couldn't have imagined the moment she'd thought he might kiss her. Yet she also knew better than anyone how not wanting to be interested was very different than actual indifference. After all, her emotions had a way of reacting without her permission.

Especially when it came to thinking about Reese.

At the information desk in the lobby of Trinity Medical Center, she asked for the room numbers of the patients she needed to see. Jamie was in the medical intensive care unit, so she decided to stop there first.

She found Jamie's bedside without difficulty. Sam entered the room, then belatedly realized a male visitor was seated next to the patient's bed.

"Oh, I'm sorry for intruding," she apologized quickly. "I didn't see you there. My name is Dr Samantha Kearn. I was the flight physician who helped transport Jamie down from Cedar Ridge."

The man bent to press a kiss to Jamie's forehead, then stood and extended his hand to greet her. "Pleased to meet you. I'm Gavin, Jamie's husband. I want to thank you for bringing her to Trinity. Although she's still very sick, the doctors here have been great. I think she's finally starting to show signs of improvement."

"I'm glad to hear it." Samantha shook his hand, then peeked at the clipboard bearing the patient's vital signs, grateful to note Jamie was indeed more stable. The patient's husband remained standing, but he reached out and took his wife's limp hand in his. She was touched by the pure devotion in Gavin's gaze as it rested on his critically ill wife.

"So, how are you holding up?" she asked him. The poor guy appeared exhausted. "You need to take care of yourself, too, you know. You won't do your wife any good by getting sick yourself."

Gavin's smile was lopsided. "You sound just like the nurses around here. They're always telling me to get more rest." His expression clouded as he gazed at his wife. "I don't think I'll be able to rest until Jamie is home with me where she belongs."

Samantha blinked back empathetic tears. For a moment the sorrow in his eyes had reminded her of the fleeting expression on Reese's face earlier. Poor Jamie and poor Gavin. Their love was obviously strong. She hoped for both of their sakes that Jamie would get better soon. "I understand. I'll come back and check in on her again in a few days."

Jamie's husband nodded and Samantha turned to leave. Next to Jamie's name on the clipboard she wrote, "critical but stable."

As she walked to the trauma ICU on the third floor, Samantha thought about her own marriage. She couldn't imagine Denis being so supportive. But she could see Reese acting very much like Gavin had, completely devoted to his wife.

A woman would be lucky to be loved like that.

She shook off the flash of self-pity and glanced down at her clipboard. What was she thinking, to be jealous of a critically ill patient? So what if Denis hadn't loved her? She had her health and her career. What more did she want? She should count her blessings.

In the trauma ICU, Sam was happy to discover how the patient who'd suffered a work-related injury, which had nearly amputated his arm, was doing well after thirty-one-hour surgery to reattach the limb. When she walked in, she found the trauma ICU nurses were packing up his supplies to move him to a regular room.

She spent a few minutes chatting with the grateful

patient. She hadn't transported him, but he remembered bits and pieces of the flight and wanted her to thank everyone who had taken care of him. She promised she would.

The last two patients on her list were already in general rooms, ready to be discharged within a few days. She jotted her notations beside their names on the clipboard and repressed the urge to go upstairs to see Jamie again. As a physician, Jamie's complicated medical course intrigued her. Sam had chosen emergency medicine for the variety, but at times like this she wondered if critical care wouldn't have been a better option. She wanted to do an in-depth chart review on Jamie's case to see if there was anything they might have missed. Not that she didn't trust the critical care team, because she did. Still, she liked taking all the signs and symptoms patients presented with and putting the puzzle pieces together until they fit into a diagnosis.

Samantha comforted herself with the knowledge Jamie was getting the best care possible. There wasn't anything more she could do for her now.

Taking the stairs to the lobby level, she headed toward the front door. Her footsteps slowed when she saw a tall blond-haired man standing near the public phone area, talking on his cell phone. She sucked in a quick breath, straining to get a look at his face. At that moment he turned, and her heart dipped when she recognized him.

Denis. What on earth was he doing here? Sweat dampened her arms beneath her turtleneck sweater and she instinctively ducked behind a tall rubber tree plant, hiding from view.

Her hands began to shake and she clasped them together tightly. Why was her ex-husband here at Trinity? Was he following her? Even if he was, did it matter? She didn't have anything to say to him.

No matter how hard he pleaded, she wasn't ever going back.

Her eyes widened when she saw Denis turn and shake hands with a gray-haired physician wearing a white lab coat. She recognized Dr Ben Harris, her boss. Why on earth would her ex-husband be meeting with the medical director of the emergency department? Denis was a pharmaceutical sales rep, but Milwaukee wasn't a part of his territory. Or at least it hadn't been while they'd been married. He'd been based in Chicago.

Though things could have easily changed since their divorce.

Her pager went off and she read the display describing a request for an ICU-to-ICU transfer. Samantha didn't want to see Denis, or talk to him, but duty won over the desire to hide. She tucked her chin into her coat, hiding behind the hood of her Lifeline jacket, and wove through the crowd to the front doors.

Outside she quickened her pace until she was almost running back to Lifeline. Reese and Andrew were waiting impatiently.

"Ready to go?" Reese asked.

"Yes." Breathlessly, she tossed aside the clipboard

and climbed into the helicopter, with Andrew close on her heels.

Once they had their helmets on and were connected to the communication system, Andrew tapped her knee to get her attention.

"How did the post-flight visits go?" he asked.

"Great. They went great." She forced herself to smile, reminding herself Denis was a part of her past, not her future. He was a pharmaceutical sales rep and for all she knew, Trinity Medical Center was part of his new territory. She simply needed to get over it.

Sam waited for Reese to finish communicating with the paramedic base to find out their destination. "So, tell me about this transport."

"Our patient is a thirty-three-year-old male who'd been snowmobiling near Two Rivers when he crashed into a tree. He lives here in Milwaukee and his family has requested he be transferred to Trinity. Apparently he has multiple fractures and will need extensive surgery and rehab, which they can't supply up there."

"He's stable, then?"

"Relatively speaking. He's suffered a serious head injury and apparently he's a smoker so his lungs aren't in the greatest shape."

Samantha nodded in understanding. "Reese? How long is the flight to Two Rivers?"

"At least an hour and a half." His deep voice rumbled through her headset. "Settle in for a long ride."

A flash of disappointment speared her heart. She normally didn't mind long flights, but in this case she'd have preferred to sit up front with Reese.

Settling back against the seat, she stared outside.

Their route was taking them over Lake Michigan. Two Rivers was located close to the coast and there was nothing but water for as far as she could see beneath them.

Twenty minutes into their ninety-minute flight, Samantha realized the air was full of snow. She leaned forward, peering out the window.

"Reese? What's with all the snow?" she asked.

"Lake effect. When the cold air meets the warmer water, the result is wet snow. I'm heading farther inland to try to avoid the worst of it. We should be fine."

Samantha tried to relax, but she couldn't help remembering how it had been weather like this that had caused the ice to form on the chopper blades. She trusted Reese implicitly, and reminded herself that worrying was useless.

An abrupt dip of the helicopter had her clutching the armrests for support.

"Everyone all right back there?" Reese's voice immediately came through her headset.

"We're fine." Samantha glanced out the window to see thick snow. "More lake-effect snow?"

"It's getting worse and the wind has kicked up dramatically. If we can't escape the worst of it by flying inland, we may have to abort." Reese's voice was grim.

Oh, boy. Samantha drew a deep breath. Never had she been in a situation where they'd had to abort a flight, but the erratic up and down movements of the helicopter were such that she wasn't about to complain. Thank heavens she didn't get airsick—at least, not that she knew of. This wasn't exactly the time she wanted to test the theory, though. "Roger. Let us know if there's something we need to do."

"Nothing right now. Just hang tight."

She was hanging tight. Sam tried to comfort herself with the knowledge that their patient was stable at Two Rivers and if they didn't get there to pick him up today, there was always the chance they could try again the next morning when the weather settled down.

Peering out the window, she couldn't see any sign of the lake or, for that matter, the shoreline. How on earth was Reese flying? Between the wind and the snow, she couldn't imagine this was any better than flying in fog.

Reese communicated with the base while she and Andrew listened. Finally, after what seemed like an hour but in reality was probably only another ten minutes, Reese made the decision to turn back.

"Base, we need to abort this flight. Visibility has dropped to below ten feet. I can't proceed safely with the wind gusts tossing us around up here like a kite."

"Roger, Lifeline, we'll notify the hospital in Two Rivers. They can either arrange for ground transport or we can try again in the morning."

"Ten-four."

Sam could tell Reese didn't like calling a halt to the transport but, looking outside, she couldn't blame him for his decision. Especially not with the wind. The safety straps of her harness dug into her shoulders and the helicopter dipped roughly again.

As much as she wanted to be able to help the patient who still needed to be transported, Sam couldn't deny she would be very glad to get both of her feet back on stable ground. If they managed to land in one piece, she was going to give Reese a big hug.

Reese's hands were slick with sweat around the stick as he finally landed the helicopter on the Lifeline helipad. For a moment he closed his eyes in relief. They'd made it. There had been several moments there when he'd had his doubts. The storm he'd read about wasn't due in until tomorrow night, but the weather over the Great Lakes was always dicey. The lake-effect snow along with the high winds had been a double whammy.

He shut down the chopper, then climbed out. Samantha and Andrew were already standing there, waiting for him. He pulled off his helmet, prepared for Samantha's wrath, when she suddenly threw her arms around his shoulders and hugged him tight.

Stunned, he didn't react quickly enough to hug her back before she stepped away. "What was that for?"

Her smile was bright and maybe a little brittle. "For getting us home safely."

A surge of protectiveness caught him unawares. Having his life in danger was bad enough, but risking Samantha's life was inconceivable. He swallowed hard and wished his hands would stop shaking.

Their shift was nearly over. Reese verified with the base they were only in red flying conditions for calls around the lakeshore. Inland calls were still a viable option.

As they split up to file their respective reports,

Reese wished for time alone with Samantha to see how she was doing. The turbulent flight must have bothered her more than she'd admitted for her to hug him like that. He couldn't afford to think her spontaneous gesture was anything more than relief.

His stomach rumbled with hunger as their lunch had been nothing more than a quick sandwich. Was Samantha hungry, too?

He was surprised by the urge to ask her out for dinner. Reese didn't date other Lifeline staff. Didn't date at all, in fact. Over the year since the crash, he'd never wanted to. His heart belonged to Valerie.

Until now. Why this sudden desire to spend time with Samantha? He could tell himself he only wanted to make sure she was okay, but that would be a lie. Oh, he did care about her state of mind, but that wasn't all. The hug had awakened every nerve ending in his body. He longed to hold her close, to stroke every inch of her creamy skin. To see if she tasted nearly as good as she looked.

After their debriefing to the next shift, Samantha prepared to leave. He quickened his pace to catch up to her, but she beat him to her car.

"Samantha, wait," he called, as she opened the driver's door.

She raised a brow. "What's the matter?"

He tucked his bare hands in the pockets of his jacket, protecting them from the cold. "I thought maybe we could get something to eat. Lunch wasn't much, if you recall." That's right, keep it simple. Friendly. This didn't have to be a date.

"Oh, er, I don't think so. But thanks for asking."

She dipped her head but he noticed a slight blush tinged her cheeks. "See you later, Reese."

"Sure. Later." For a moment he stood there and watched her as she slid behind the wheel and dutifully put on her seat belt. Since they both lived in the same complex, he decided to follow her home. He quickly climbed into his truck before she could leave without him.

Only she didn't. When he realized there was something wrong, he left the warm interior of his truck to brave the cold. He tapped on her window. "What's wrong?"

She reluctantly opened the door. "My car won't start." Frustration laced her tone.

"Battery?" he suggested, poking his head inside. He could problem-solve helicopter engines much easier than car engines. And it was too cold to stand out here for long. "Did you leave a light on?"

"I don't think so. Could be my battery needs to be replaced, though. I think my mechanic mentioned something to that effect last year." Samantha curled her fists. "I'll have to call a tow truck."

"Why don't you let me take you home?" Reese quickly offered. Why jump-start her car when he could spend time with her instead? "Then we'll see about your car."

She didn't want to go with him, that much was obvious. Samantha stared out through the windshield for so long he had to stamp his feet to keep his toes from freezing in the chilly air. Maybe he should have simply fetched his jumper cables. Car trouble wasn't the end of the world. This was just a friendly offer to help and he was about to say so when she finally nodded.

"Sure. I guess you can take me home."

Clearly she didn't like the idea of leaving her car, and while he sympathized with her plight he couldn't help pushing his luck. "And dinner? I mean, hey, we need to eat, right?"

With a wry grin she eyed him suspiciously. "If I didn't know better, I'd think you sabotaged my car on purpose."

His eyes widened in horror. "I didn't!"

She laughed at his reaction. "I know. All right, dinner, too."

Hot damn. Reese couldn't prevent a huge grin spreading over his features. Maybe he was a fool, but he hadn't looked forward to spending time with a beautiful woman in what seemed like forever. Ignoring the warning signals bleeping urgently in his brain, he opened her door and offered his hand. She hesitated only for a moment, a motion so slight he would have missed it if he hadn't been so in tune with her every nuance.

Then she placed her ungloved hand in his. He liked the feel of her small, strong, very capable hand. Awed by her trust, he slowly drew her to her feet. In that moment, he knew his fate was sealed.

He could no longer stay away from Samantha any more than he could give up flying.

CHAPTER SIX

SAM knew she was in trouble when Reese's warm fingers curled firmly around hers. This deliberate touch seemed much different than the impulsive hug she'd bestowed on him earlier. Despite the cold, heat skipped along the nerve endings in her arm. When they were flying together, his voice was a rudder in a rock-filled sea. But now his touch heightened the sense of an impending storm. She needed to pull away, to establish some space between them.

Heck, she needed to breathe.

His truck was parked right next to her car, so he didn't hold her hand for long. As soon as he'd tucked her into the passenger seat, he slammed the door and jogged around the truck to slide in beside her.

There, much better. Or so she thought, until he turned the key in the ignition and turned toward her. He was close. Much too close. "So, what are you in the mood for?"

You. She bit her tongue to prevent herself from blurting out the ridiculous truth. Food. He'd meant, what was she in the mood for as far as food went.

Nibbling on him wasn't an option.

"Er, really, I don't care. Whatever you feel like is fine with me." The way her stomach clenched, she doubted she'd be able to eat anything, no matter what he chose.

In the dark interior of the truck she couldn't read his expression. "Chinese take-out?" His voice held a distinct note of hopefulness.

She took pity on him. "Sure, sounds good."

"You like Chinese?" He divided his attention between her and the road.

"Doesn't everyone?" She clasped her hands in her lap to keep them warm. The air blasting through his vents was still frigid. She should have worn her gloves.

"Not necessarily," Reese argued softly. "I tend to have an adventurous appetite."

"Really?" Sam wondered what sort of appetite he meant, food or something more? "So what's your favorite Chinese dish?"

"Yu-Hsing chicken, but a lot of places don't have it. I'm not picky, though. Anything wrapped in an egg roll works for me."

She tilted her head to look at him. She'd gotten the impression he'd been at Lifeline for a while, but she didn't know much about Reese's past or the secrets he might have buried. "Have you actually been there? To China?"

"Nah." He flashed her a quick, lethal grin. "I just like to eat. I'm the guy who goes to an ethnic restaurant and orders whatever the house specialty is. You'd be amazed at the weird stuff I've eaten."

"Don't tell me," she joked, raising a hand in warning. "I don't want to ruin my appetite."

Reese stopped at a small Chinese restaurant a few blocks from their apartment complex which she hadn't even known existed. She offered to wait in the car but he dragged her inside, forcing her to help pick out food. When they had enough white boxes to feed half the population of Hong Kong, he carried them outside, then stashed them in the back seat.

A spicy scent filled the interior of the truck, making her mouth water with anticipation as they drove. Soon the Oak Terrace apartment buildings loomed into view. He paused at the fork in the road. "Your place or mine?"

"Mine." Her breath caught in her throat as he turned into the drive leading to the North building. She wanted to place a hand over her racing heart. Good grief, she needed to calm down. This was only dinner. She hadn't agreed to sleep with him, for heaven's sake.

Although inviting Reese into the intimacy of her apartment put all kinds of shocking ideas into her head. Not one of them had anything to do with sleep.

Reese carried the huge bag holding their dinner as he followed her inside. Sam glanced around the interior of her apartment, reassuring herself the place was reasonably neat, before opening the door wide to let him in.

"I'll call a friend of mine who owns a garage to see about your car, if you don't mind opening boxes." He set the bag on the table.

"Of course not." Samantha willed her fingers to stop trembling as she pulled several containers out of the bag and began to open them. Surely she could share a meal with a friend without making a big deal out of the situation. She listened as Reese gave his buddy the details about her car, including the directions to her apartment to get the keys. She pulled plates, silverware and glasses out of the cupboard, set them on the table, then glanced around her stark apartment with dismay. What she wouldn't give for a little background music. Unfortunately, she'd left her previous apartment in a hurry and hadn't bothered to take her small sound system with her.

Time to purchase a new one, then. Another small step to getting her personal life in order.

Reese hung up and eyed the spread of steaming white boxes on the table with glee. If he noticed the barren walls and lack of interior decorating of her living space, he didn't comment. "Looks great."

"Dig in," she invited. Her eyes widened as Reese heaped food on his plate, taking a sampling from every single container. He still wore his flight suit from work and she wondered where on his lean frame he would put all the food.

When she spooned sweet and sour chicken and broccoli onto her rice, her appetite returned with a vengeance.

"I was hungrier than I realized," she admitted a few minutes later, taking a break from her meal.

Reese's brown eyes darkened as his gaze met hers. "Lately, it seems I'm hungrier than I realized, too."

There was no mistaking his meaning. Samantha's hand froze halfway to her mouth and a big drop of sweet and sour sauce plopped on the table beneath her fork. She swallowed hard and dabbed at the spot with her napkin.

Tension shimmered between them. Oh, boy, she

was in over her head. Way over. The silence was deafening.

Until her doorbell buzzed loudly. She started, her fork clattering to her plate.

"Must be Vince." Reese nonchalantly stood, as if he hadn't tried to singe her with his heated gaze. "I need to give him your keys."

"What? Oh, uh, sure." She fumbled with her purse until she fished them out and handed them over. Damn, she hated feeling like a green medical student at her first autopsy. She was almost a board-certified emergency medical physician. About time she acted like one. She was in control of her life and planned to stay that way.

In a matter of minutes Reese had given Vince her keys with instructions to call him in the morning on the status of her car. Vince left with a cheerful wave. Sam resisted the urge to call him back.

Reese shut the door behind him. "So, where were we?"

"We were eating a friendly dinner." She added a little emphasis to the word "friendly."

"Of course." He returned to his seat. "Everything tastes wonderful."

"Yeah, I slaved all day over a hot stove." Sam rolled her eyes and pushed her plate away. "Thanks for calling Vince to take care of my car."

"No problem." Reese ate until he'd cleaned every last speck of rice from his plate. She couldn't remember when she'd enjoyed watching a man eat. Reese might consider himself adventurous but Denis had quirky tastes when it came to food. He would only eat certain things prepared a specific way. And more often than not he'd claimed she'd done it wrong.

Whoa, enough of those thoughts. Sam stood and began to close the boxes that still contained food. "You're going to have to take these leftovers with you. I'll never be able to eat all this."

"Yum, breakfast."

His wide, innocent gaze didn't fool her in the least. They weren't going to share breakfast. Her gaze narrowed. "I'm sure there's enough here for your breakfast, lunch and dinner."

"I bet you're right." He caught her hand as she placed a box in the original bag. "Thank you, Samantha."

She went still, caught off guard by his obvious sincerity. "For what?"

"For sharing dinner with me." His thumb lightly stroked the back of her hand.

"You're welcome." Sam needed to sit or, as God was her witness, she'd fall flat on her face. Reese slowly stood, still claiming her hand. When he stepped closer, she sensed his intent and told herself to step back, out of reach.

Her feet didn't listen to her brain's feeble command. As if she were a puppet dangling from a string, she watched him lean toward her. His mouth brushed hers, lightly at first as if testing the water, then, when she didn't pull away, he kissed her again.

Deeper. Hungrily. His mouth possessed hers. Heat flared, hot and needy. She wrapped her arms around his lean waist. Before her head stopped spinning he abruptly ended the kiss, dragging his hands from her shoulders to her arms. She reluctantly let him go.

His voice was low and husky with desire as he stepped away. "I'd better go, while I still can."

No, her body screamed in protest. Yes, her mind insisted.

He'd almost made it to her door before she stopped him. "Reese."

He swung around to face her. "Yeah?"

"I...don't think I'm ready for a relationship." The words came out in a rush, but it was only fair to warn him. As wonderfully nice as he was, this thing, whatever it was between them, couldn't go anywhere.

His smile was crooked. "I know. Me neither. Except I think it's too late."

"Too late?" What on earth did he mean?

"I don't seem to have a choice where you're concerned."

Her dismay must have shone in her eyes, because he quickly smiled. "Hey, there's no need to panic. Just promise me one thing."

"If I can," she hedged. Her fingers curled around one of her kitchen chairs for support. She didn't give promises lightly. Not anymore.

"Promise you'll let me help keep you safe, at least for the next few months until you finish your training at Lifeline." His gaze turned somber. "As a friend, Samantha, if that's what you prefer. Once you graduate from training, I'll let you go."

Madness. What he'd proposed was sheer madness. She wasn't in any real danger other than some of the routine risks of her job. The last thing her heart needed was to be tangled up with another man. Even more, she couldn't afford to give up her newfound independence. Reese had no idea how much he was asking of her.

"I don't know if I can," she confessed.

"Just think about it. I'd never ask for more than you're willing to give." He opened her apartment door. "Goodnight, Samantha."

She didn't want him to go, but forced herself to stay where she was, far too tempted to reach out to the man whose strength drew her as much as the glimmer of sorrow in his eyes. He was long gone before she answered in a quiet voice, "Goodnight, Reese."

Reese didn't remember much about getting home. He hadn't had any wine but he felt light-headed and fuzzy as if he'd drunk several bottles all by himself.

He could still taste Samantha on his lips. Could see the wide, dazed expression in her eyes when he'd lifted his mouth from hers. With a groan he stared up at the ceiling of his bedroom, his lower body hard and aching.

Cripes, he wanted her. In a way he hadn't wanted a woman in a long time. She wasn't ready for a relationship. A rusty laugh strangled in his throat. Hell, he could relate to that. But he'd told her the truth. He'd sworn not to get involved, yet here he was, tangled into knots over a tiny redheaded flight physician. Tumbling headfirst into what certainly resembled a relationship, pitfalls and all.

With an effort he pulled himself away from that line of thinking. Samantha wasn't ready for a relationship, so he'd honor the terms of his proposition. He simply wanted her to be safe, at least while she was flying in his care.

Surely they could remain friends, at least until she'd finished her training.

He must have drifted into sleep at some point during the wee hours of the morning because when he abruptly opened his eyes, bright light poured through the window of his bedroom.

Blinking, he peered outside. The temperature was probably well below freezing but the sunlight sure gave the impression of warmth. A perfect day to spend outside. And on his day off, too. What would Samantha say if he proposed a little outing?

The ringing of his phone distracted him from thoughts of Samantha. Praying there wasn't some problem at Lifeline, he warily picked up the receiver. "Yeah?"

"Reese?"

"Hey, Vince." He relaxed at the sound of his friend's voice and padded to the kitchen. "What's up? Don't tell me you've already looked at Samantha's car?"

"As a matter of fact, I did."

"So was it the battery? She thought it might need to be replaced." Reese tucked the phone between his shoulder and his ear so he could dig the leftover Chinese food out of the fridge. He never minded eating leftovers, although they would have tasted far better if Samantha were here to share them.

"Sort of."

Reese frowned as he opened the cartons. Vince's tone was weird, evasive. "What do you mean, sort of? Samantha's car trouble is either a result of a defunct battery or not."

"The battery is defunct all right. Although not by accident."

A shiver of dread slithered down his spine. "Someone messed with her battery on purpose? How can you tell?"

"Gee, maybe by the round indentations made by a hammerhead where it smashed her battery? Acid leaked all over, creating a hell of a mess."

"A hammer." Reese sank into a chair, tunneled his fingers through his hair. "I bet her ex, that damn Markowicz, wrecked her battery on purpose."

"Yeah, that's my assessment. What's the deal? Do you know this guy Markowicz?"

"No." But he'd sure like to. The flower delivery had been annoying but basically harmless. Smashing a battery with a hammer turned the violence up a notch. "Can you fix it?"

"Yeah, shouldn't be too bad. I'll have to replace the battery, of course. Cleaning up the interior where the acid leaked all over will be the hardest part. Can't tell you for sure what parts the acid may have ruined until I dig into the engine."

"Do what you can." Reese toyed with the carton of Chinese food. His hearty appetite had seemingly vanished. "Send the bill to me."

"Sure thing." Vince hesitated. "Do you want me to call Samantha so I can tell her what happened?"

"No, I'll do it." His stomach clenched at the

thought. "Just work on getting her car fixed as soon as possible."

"Will do."

Reese hung up the phone. First, he'd shower then go over to find Samantha. There wasn't going to be an easy way to soften this blow. Better if he told her in person.

His hair was still damp from the shower when his doorbell buzzed. Wearing only his jeans and a long-sleeved T-shirt, he crossed to the intercom. "Who is it?"

"Samantha."

"Come on in." Surprised, he pushed the button releasing the lock on the outside door. What had brought Samantha over here? Had she somehow found out the news about her car from Vince?

He opened his apartment door, watching her walk down the hallway toward him. Like him, she was dressed casually in blue jeans. Although she wore a bulky jacket, he could see she wore another of those turtleneck sweaters, this one in bright green.

Maybe he had a weird neck fetish.

"Good morning. Did you walk over from your place?"

"Yes, it's not far." Samantha didn't smile at him—in fact, her pretty brow was furrowed in a frown. "I came over to get Vince's phone number. I should have asked for the information last night, before you left."

"Come on in." Reese gestured for her to come inside. "I already spoke to Vince."

Her frown deepened. "That's very nice of you, but I'd rather take care of this myself. It's my car. I'm sure I can arrange to get it repaired."

Well, hell. What had caused this change of heart? Reese stood awkwardly in his bare feet. "Are you hungry?" Stalling, he turned back toward the Chinese food he'd left on the table. "We can eat breakfast."

"No, thanks." Samantha remained where she was, standing near his doorway as if she'd bolt if given half the chance. "If you'd just give me Vince's phone number, I'll be out of your hair."

He didn't think she'd appreciate knowing he liked having her in his hair. And in his apartment. Better not to think of how fantastic she'd look in his bed. Dragging his thoughts away from that scenario, he noticed her firm stance at his door. With a sigh, he realized she wasn't going to make this easy. "Samantha, there's no easy way to tell you, but your car trouble wasn't an accident."

Her wary gaze sharpened. "What do you mean?"

"Sit down. Please," he added, when she didn't move.

"Denis did something to my car, didn't he?" She crossed her arms protectively over her chest.

"Yes." Reese couldn't see the point in lying to her. "He smashed your battery and it leaked acid all over your engine. I authorized Vince to do the repairs. He's going to get your car fixed as soon as possible."

"You authorized Vince to do the repairs?" Her voice was dangerously soft.

He didn't understand her strange reaction. Why wasn't she more worried about her ex's tendency to violence? Instead, she seemed annoyed with him. She had been happy enough with his help last night. "Yes. Don't worry, I'll take care of everything."

"No, you won't." Samantha glared at him, fury spiking her stormy gray eyes. Wow, had he ever seen her angry? "Give me Vince's number. I don't need people like you taking control. I'm better off taking care of things myself."

CHAPTER SEVEN

SAMANTHA'S entire body vibrated with suppressed fury. Why had she caved in under the pressure and accepted help from Reese last night? She should have known better than to rely on a man. Reese was a bulldozer, just like Denis. One tiny favor and he acted as if he owned her.

Oh, God. Never again.

She straightened her spine, prepared to fight. But instead Reese simply went over to his phone, jotted Vince's number on a slip of paper and crossed the room to hand it to her.

"I'm sorry. You're absolutely right. It's your car. I should have asked Vince to call you first thing."

His quiet apology caught her off guard. Again. Damn it, why couldn't he stay true to form? It was easier to resent him when he was being a jerk. And why couldn't he put socks on his feet? She fought to keep her voice steady. "Yes, you should have."

"You're not helpless, Samantha. I know how well you take care of everything. Hell, you literally save lives every day. I just wanted to help. Kind of the way I help by flying you to places where you can do the most good."

The earnest expression in his warm brown eyes made it difficult to hang on to her anger. His damp mink-colored hair curling around his ears and his bare toes didn't help either. Since when had she noticed a man's toes? With a sigh, she took Vince's number and nodded.

"I know." She turned to leave.

"Are you sure you won't stay for breakfast?" His voice stopped her as she opened his door. "I can whip up an omelet if you like."

"No, but thanks." She lifted her hand in a simple wave. "See you later."

She thought she heard him say something like, "Count on it," before she closed the door behind her.

Sam lifted her face to the sun as she stepped outside. The warmth after several days of sub-zero temperatures felt wonderful. The walk from Reese's building to hers wasn't far and she was proud of the way she didn't glance over her shoulder every ten seconds, looking for Denis the Menace.

Why had he smashed her car battery? Was this more of his need for control? He'd often used words as weapons, but breaking things was out of character. What would he break next? She couldn't even begin to guess. Denis wasn't always ruled by logic.

Even with this new turn of events she was still royally ticked at herself for having allowed Reese to take over her car problems last night in the first place. Thoughts of sharing more than a meal with him had obviously clouded her judgment. Well, no more. She would call Vince, making it very clear she was in charge of her car repairs and the bill. Reese was not. He was a nice guy, but if she didn't maintain her independence, what did she have?

Loneliness.

For a moment, her shoulders slumped. How many times over the past year had she wished for someone to lean on? Her family was on the other side of the continent and keeping close friends during a medical residency wasn't easy. Every month she was shipped off to a new rotation, with a whole new group of other residents. At least, that had been the pattern until this last stint at Lifeline.

Lifeline didn't change residents every month, mostly because of the lengthy flight training. Also, because she'd requested a double rotation. Ben Harris had been more than willing to juggle the schedule in her favor.

Had Denis really contacted Ben because of her? She shied away from the thought. Denis had probably had a business appointment with Ben. For all she knew, his sales territory had been changed to include Milwaukee. There was no reason to think a pharmaceutical sales rep had a special friendship with her boss. She didn't envy Denis's job. As a rule, most of the physicians didn't do much more than tolerate sales reps. They were sources of free food and free drug samples and that was all. Most physicians resented the high cost of pharmaceuticals and didn't hesitate to let the sales reps know of their displeasure.

The fact that Denis hadn't made it through medical school only worked against him. She knew firsthand how much he resented all physicians for accomplishing something he hadn't been able to.

Her success had pushed Denis over the edge. When she'd started her residency training, she'd noticed his behavior had changed. And not for the better.

With a start Sam realized she'd arrived at her apartment building. The weather was so nice, she was tempted to keep walking. Too bad she didn't have her car, or she would consider heading downtown to the lakefront. Wasn't there some sort of Winterfest going on this weekend? How long had it been since she'd done anything for fun?

"Samantha."

Heart pounding, she whirled at the sound of her name. Her breath whooshed out of her lungs when she saw Reese standing a few feet behind her, his hands tucked into his pockets. "Darn it. Don't do that to me."

"I'm sorry. I called your name earlier but you didn't hear me." His dark eyes held regret.

She forced a smile. Her jumpiness wasn't Reese's fault. "I guess I was deep in thought."

He didn't ask about what. Knowing Reese, he could no doubt guess. Amazing when she thought about it. Reese knew more about her personal life than anyone.

"Would you be interested in going down to Winterfest with me? We're both off and it's such an unusually nice day, it seems a shame to waste it."

How had he read her mind? Sam's first instinct was to refuse, but the alternative of going back to her closed-in, sterile apartment held no appeal. "I have to call Vince," she told him, which wasn't an answer at all.

"I know. I'll wait."

Still, Sam hesitated. She didn't want to give Reese the wrong impression, but then again she had made her feelings about relationships very clear. What could it hurt to go down to Winterfest with him? When was the last time she'd had the luxury of going out with a friend?

"All right." She decided quickly, before she could analyze things to death and find a reason to talk herself out of going. "Give me a few minutes and I'll be back out."

A ghost of a smile flitted across Reese's features. "I'll get my truck and wait for you."

Sam nodded and quickly dashed inside. She called Vince, but had to leave a message. Not a big deal, since she knew darned well Reese had already talked to him. With excitement flickering through her veins, she spent a few purely adolescent minutes in front of the mirror, then grabbed her purse and headed back outside.

When she jumped in the truck beside Reese, he flashed her a warm smile. Maybe, with Reese's help, she could forget all about Denis, at least for a little while.

The lakefront teemed with life, people everywhere walking and jogging. Partially because of the Winterfest activities, including a giant ice sculpture contest taking place right on the shores of Lake Michigan, but more so, she guessed, because of the unseasonably warm weather. Not that temperatures close to forty were exactly warm, but winter in Wisconsin was cold. Like really, really cold. Which made temperatures in the forties more than tolerable.

There was a huge banner announcing a Children's

Memorial Hospital Fund-raiser being held in a few weeks at the Lakefront Art Museum. The tickets were expensive, although the money was for a good cause. Too costly for her budget, but she wondered if Lifeline would spring for them? She made a mental note to look into it before she and Reese wandered toward the ice sculpture display.

"Will you look at that?" Reese stopped in front of a guy teetering on a stepladder, intently carving his massive ice sculpture of a hot-air balloon. "Very cool."

Sam raised a brow. "Did you always dream of flying, even as a kid?"

Reese didn't take his eyes off the hot-air balloon emerging from the block of ice. "Yeah, pretty much. But mostly I was fixated on planes. All sorts of planes. I joined the Air Force straight out of high school, just so I could learn to fly planes."

"So how did you end up flying helicopters?"

He turned toward her and shrugged. "Couldn't afford to be picky. They needed chopper pilots so that's the track they sent me. Since I was learning to fly, I wasn't about to complain. And I quickly learned to love the flexibility of the whirlybirds. You can't set a big hulking plane down on a dime."

She could easily imagine Reese in the military. He had a quiet strength that must have helped him endure the tough physical training as well as the constant rules and regulations. She wanted to know more—about his parents, his family, where he grew up. But before she could figure out a non-nosy way to ask, as they wandered amongst the ice sculpture displays, his hand smoothly captured hers.

She enjoyed the protective feeling of his hand around hers and knew she should consider pulling away. Wasn't hand-holding a violation of the friendship agreement? His hand was nice, warm and firm without being too tight around hers. For the life of her, she couldn't bear to give up the slight contact.

He'd promised not to ask for more than she was willing to give and she couldn't help but believe Reese was the type of guy who kept his promises.

"What about this one?" she asked, pausing in front of a giant ice beetle. "What makes someone want to carve a bug?"

"I don't know, but I like the race car over there." Reese gestured with his hand to the sculpture up ahead. "It's true to scale. I feel like I could jump inside and take a spin."

"Men and their toys," she teased.

"How about some lunch?" Reese asked as they came up alongside a couple of fast-food vendors. "I bet you didn't eat breakfast either."

She hadn't and knew her refusal to stay and eat with him had probably caused him to miss his breakfast too since he hadn't wasted any time in following her this morning. "Sure, but I don't want to wait in line. I'd like to sit and look out over the water for a bit."

"Tell me what you want, and I'll bring it over," Reese promised.

She made her selection—hot, spicy, Cajun chicken—then ambled toward the shore. The rhythmic sound of waves crashing over the rocks was almost as soothing as Reese's voice flowing through her headset in flight.

Squealing tires, followed by a loud thump, made her turn with a frown. Screams split the air.

"Oh, my God, he's hit. *He's hit!*"

Before the woman's screams fully registered, Samantha was running toward the group huddled by the side of the road. She quickly shoved her way through the crowd.

"I'm a doctor. Let me through."

Like a parting of the sea, people moved out of her way. She instantly saw the victim, a man who appeared to be in his late twenties or early thirties dressed in jogging clothes, sprawled along the side of the road. Blood trickled from a wound on his temple and the odd angle of his legs had her suspecting a pelvic fracture at the very least.

"Someone call 911," she directed in a stern voice as she knelt at the victim's side.

"I did." Reese materialized by her side. "Do you need help?"

"Not yet." Samantha positioned the man's head to open his airway. He wasn't breathing. Before she could pull a small resuscitation mask from her purse, Reese handed her one.

"Here, I carry one at all times."

Grateful, she took the mask and used it to give the victim rescue breaths. Then, following the ABCs just like they did in the ED, she checked for a pulse.

"No pulse," she muttered, before placing her

hands over the sternum to perform chest compressions.

"I'll breathe for you." Reese positioned himself at the patient's head.

Good thing the pilots at Lifeline were trained in CPR. Samantha concentrated on performing good chest compressions, counting out loud so Reese would know when to give a breath. They worked together in tandem as if they'd done this a hundred times before.

"Pulse check," Samantha suggested. "First with compressions." A little trick she'd learned in medical school, when you could feel the pulse with chest compressions, it was easier to then stop them to see if there was a spontaneous return of the victim's pulse.

"Pulse good with compressions," Reese informed her.

"Okay. What about now?" She halted her compressions, waiting while he kept his hand in the same place along the carotid artery. She waited a moment, knowing how easy it was to miss a pulse on a victim when your own was pumping in double time.

"No pulse. Continue CPR."

Samantha nodded and began the chest compression routine all over again.

She and Reese had performed several rounds of CPR before she heard the distinct wail of sirens. She wished for a chance to do a neuro exam on the patient, but if they didn't maintain his oxygenation with breathing and chest compressions, there wouldn't be a neuro status to worry about.

The paramedics arrived on the scene and quickly

took over the rescue breathing with an oxygen tank and ambu-bag. Samantha didn't let up on her chest compressions as they made the switch.

"Are you all right there for a while longer?" one of the paramedics wanted to know.

She nodded. "I'm an emergency medicine resident working at Lifeline," she informed them.

The paramedics nodded, trusting her skills. Once they had the patient connected to the portable monitoring equipment, she stopped compressions so they could see the underlying rhythm. Seeing V-fib, they shocked him. Once, twice, then a third time.

When those shocks didn't convert him, they quickly intubated the patient and flushed medication straight down his endotracheal tube directly into his lungs. They worked over him for another ten minutes, giving more meds and shocking again.

"He's converted into sinus rhythm," one of the paramedics noted. "Let's get him into the truck."

The paramedics didn't waste a second but packed him up and whisked him off, presumably to Trinity Medical Center. Samantha stood there, watching them drive away, feeling at a loss. Normally she would be on the receiving end of getting this patient from the field. Being the first responder on the scene felt extremely odd.

"You were amazing." Reese came up behind her and gently squeezed her shoulders. "You saved his life."

"*We* saved his life," she corrected, slanting him a wry look over her shoulder. The need to lose herself in Reese's arms was strong. "Thanks for your help.

I really hope he makes it. At least he has youth on his side."

"If he doesn't, it's not because we didn't do our best," Reese observed quietly. He slowly turned her so she was facing him. He reached up to tuck a strand of hair behind her ear.

"I know." She tried to smile. But the intense expression in Reese's eyes practically sent her heart into V-tach. Before she could think of protesting, he pulled her close.

"Samantha." He didn't try to kiss her, but tucked her head into the hollow of his shoulder. "This time I think we both need a hug."

She closed her eyes and inhaled the comforting scent of his spicy aftershave. He held her close, but not so hard that she felt as if she were suffocating. His chest was firm, muscular and yet, oh, so soft.

"Excuse me," a strange voice interrupted them. "I need to ask you a few questions."

Sam raised her head to find a Milwaukee police officer standing beside them. "Of course," she responded.

Reese prevented her from breaking free of his embrace, but tucked an arm over her shoulder so they could face the officer together. "What can we do for you?"

"Did you see the car that hit him?"

Samantha slowly shook her head. "No, but I heard the screech of the tires and the thud as he was hit."

"That's what I was afraid of. Only one woman saw a brown car slam on the brakes and hit the jogger, but she didn't get the make of the car or the number off the plates.''

For a moment, Sam didn't understand. ''You mean, this was a hit-and-run?''

The officer's expression was grim. ''Yes. And we don't have a clue to point us in the direction of the assailant.''

CHAPTER EIGHT

REESE frowned and swept a glance around the area. "Someone must have seen something."

"I hope so." The cop's tone didn't sound overly optimistic. "If you remember anything, let me know." He moved on, to question the next person.

The cheerful, carefree atmosphere at the lakefront turned somber. Several strangers came up to congratulate them on working so hard to save the victim's life. Reese finally drew Samantha away from the crowd, sensing her impatience with the attention.

"I was just doing my job," she muttered under her breath. "You'd think these people would understand that."

"You were awesome," Reese corrected softly. "And most of these folks don't see that kind of action except on television."

"I guess." She didn't sound satisfied.

"Hungry?" Reese doubted it, but his own stomach was rumbling like mad. "I really gotta get something to eat."

"Sure, we can eat something." This time, though, she stood in line beside him. They took their meal over to a large boulder overlooking the lake. The rippling blue water shimmered beneath the sun.

He noticed Samantha didn't do much more than pick at her Cajun chicken, but he figured a little food was better than nothing. His appetite was indestructible, enabling him to devour his burger quickly.

The wind picked up, putting a definite chill in the air. He convinced her to walk through the rest of the ice sculpture displays, but even when the hot-air balloon won first place, her heart wasn't into celebrating.

Reese couldn't blame her. He'd been impressed with her calm professionalism during their rescue efforts. She was the one in need of protecting, yet she willingly saved lives every day. While he knew her ex couldn't have had anything to do with the hit-and-run accident, especially since the jogger hadn't been anywhere near Samantha when he'd been hit, the image of the guy lying bleeding in the street, his leg obviously broken, wouldn't leave him alone. He suspected Markowicz was bothering Samantha. He didn't want to think of what might happen if her ex turned his violence toward her.

"I think I'm ready to head home." Samantha shivered and buried her face in the warmth of her coat. "It suddenly seems cold out here."

"Yeah, I know." He glanced at his watch, then steered them in the direction of where he'd parked his truck. "But it's still early enough to get in touch with Vince. We might be able to pick up your car on the way home." He remembered her annoyance with him earlier that morning. "If you were planning to pick it up today, that is," he hastily added. "If not, that's okay, too."

"I was hoping to pick it up today." She arched a brow at him. "I suppose you just happen to have Vince's number handy, too, I bet."

"Yeah." He gave her a cautious glance as he unlocked the truck. Heaven knew, he felt as if he were walking through a minefield. With Samantha, he was quickly beginning to realize that offering to help resembled a cardinal sin. "Why, does that make you mad?"

"No." She blew out her breath in exasperation. "I guess not. Okay, give me the number. I'll use my cell phone."

Reese rattled off the number as she punched it into her cell phone. He listened to her one-sided conversation and was glad when it sounded as if Vince did indeed have her car running again.

"To Vince's auto shop?" he asked, when she'd turned off her phone.

"Sure." She stared out of the windshield with a frown. "What's with all the traffic?"

"The Bucks game is at home tonight." Something he should have thought of, they could have avoided much of the traffic by leaving a little earlier. He slanted her a glance. "Not much of a basketball fan?" he guessed.

She shrugged. "I don't really have a lot of time for sports. Probably won't until after I pass my boards."

Over the past year at Lifeline, he'd learned the senior emergency medicine residents were scheduled to take their medical boards in June. It was only February now. "You've already started studying?"

"Well, they're not something you can cram for." Her dry humor made him smile.

"I guess not. I'm amazed you can concentrate at

all with everything that's going on in your personal life." Damn Markowicz anyway. Didn't he know this was an important time for her?

"I'm used to it." She looked away and he instinctively knew the subject was closed. Maybe she was used to it, but she shouldn't have to be. Reese wished, more than anything, he could get Markowicz alone, just for a couple of minutes.

The traffic jam broke up after a few miles. He headed straight for Vince's garage. Although it was difficult, he remained in the car while she spoke with Vince, watching as they both poked their heads under the hood while Vince pointed out the items he'd fixed or replaced.

Reese wanted to see the damaged battery for himself. But if he got out and demanded Vince show him, Samantha would expect to inspect the damage as well. After the earlier hit-and-run accident, he figured she didn't need to see any reminders of violence.

She paid Vince, then waved at Reese as she climbed into her car. He didn't want the evening to end. His problem, of course, he acknowledged as he followed her home. When he pulled up and parked next to her, she shot him an exasperated glance.

"You're off duty, now, Reese." She slammed her car door with a little too much force. "I don't need a baby-sitter."

Reese shook his head. "I'm not volunteering for baby-sitting duty. Please, Samantha, I just want to walk you to your door." And follow her inside. But he kept that thought to himself.

"What, no offer of dinner?" She crossed her arms over her chest. "I'm shocked."

Since he had, in fact, been about to offer to order pizza, he clamped his jaw shut. "I don't know how anyone can forget to eat," he muttered as they walked up to the door.

"I don't forget, I just don't have your metabolism," she pointed out as she dug for her key. "Thanks for taking me to Winterfest, Reese." She flashed him a smile. "It certainly was an adventure."

He wasn't blind; the expression on her pretty face clearly indicated she wanted him to leave. Yet he had no intention of following her wishes. "All the way in, Samantha."

For a moment he wondered if he'd pushed a little too hard. Safety wasn't anything to take lightly. He knew only too well what carelessness could bring. Damn, but the woman could be stubborn when she wanted.

"Fine, come on in, then." Annoyed, she used her key to open the door. "Anyone ever tell you you're persistent?"

"Like you should talk." He held the door, then followed her inside. "What's the harm of me walking you in? I'm not about to jump your bones, although they are very lovely bones."

Shocked, she glared at him. "I never said you would."

He kept his eyes wide, innocent. "Then what's the problem?"

"You're the problem." Samantha used her key to unlock the door of her apartment and, much like the last time, she opened it wide so he could look in. "See? Everything is fine. Goodnight, Reese."

"What's that?" A white slip of paper caught his eye, partially hidden beneath the door. He bent over, pulled it out, then straightened. Words were printed in large block letters. COME HOME, OR YOU'RE NEXT.

"Oh, God. Denis." Samantha paled and Reese swore the only thing keeping her upright was the door at her back.

A red haze of anger blurred his vision. He blocked the fury with an effort. "This is an outright threat. You're not staying here. I'm taking you to my place."

"No, I'm not leaving." She looked like she might faint but her tone was steady.

Incredulous, he stared at her. "You can't be serious. Read this. Do you know what it means? You're next? Next for what, Samantha? Another hit-and-run accident?"

"He was there, wasn't he? He must have seen the accident. He saw us together." Samantha's voice was hoarse.

Gentling his tone, he agreed, "Yes, so that's why you need to come to my place with me. Do you want to pack a bag?"

"No, Reese." Samantha was so pale, her gray eyes looked like dark stormclouds in a sea of white. "I appreciate what you're trying to do, but he's not chasing me out of my home."

"Then I'm not leaving." He followed her inside the apartment, closing the door behind him. "Not until you've called the police."

Relief flooded him when she seemingly ignored him, heading for her phone. Reese scrubbed a hand along his jaw as Samantha called the police. He hadn't wanted the evening to end, but extending the time he could spend with her because of something like this wasn't what he'd wanted either.

Safety, at least for Samantha, seemed more elusive than ever.

Sam was freezing. She wore a turtleneck sweater and the thermostat in her apartment was cranked to seventy-five degrees, but she was still cold.

She didn't want to believe Denis had followed her down to the lakefront. Why hadn't she felt his presence? A shiver tore through her. Maybe she hadn't noticed because of Reese, but the notion didn't make her feel any better. Denis had been jealously possessive without the least bit of provocation on her part. They were divorced, but she could only imagine what had gone through his mind when he'd seen Reese walking beside her, holding her hand.

The police were on their way but Samantha didn't hold out much hope of the investigation helping to prove Denis was behind the note. Knowing Reese was probably hungry again, she offered to throw something together for dinner.

"Why don't I just order out for pizza?" he suggested.

"Sure." She lifted a shoulder. It didn't matter what he ordered, food wasn't high on her list of priorities at the moment.

The pizza arrived before the police did. Reese was

annoyed with the fact, but Sam understood. Unfortunately, this was how the system worked. The threat wasn't immediate, there was no need to rush.

When the officer arrived, she gestured to the note. Reese had picked it up, but she'd refused to touch it.

"What time did you leave this morning?" The officer wanted to know.

She had no idea. With a raised brow, she glanced at Reese. "Close to ten-thirty," he responded.

The officer wanted to hear everything that had transpired throughout the day. Samantha condensed the events the best she could and explained about the restraining order. When the officer questioned her about the previous threats, Reese lost his temper.

"Dammit, you should already know about the previous threats! Didn't she just tell you about the restraining order? How many threats before you take this seriously? For God's sake, it's no wonder you can't find this guy."

The officer wasn't amused. "I am taking this seriously and we'll file a report. There isn't much more we can do. A restraining order doesn't mean anything without proof. We don't have the manpower to follow Markowicz around every place he goes." The officer turned his attention back to Samantha. "We can put a tap on your phone, drive by more often and see if we can get a glimpse of him violating the agreement. That's about all."

Reese continued to mutter but Samantha knew the officer was right. Unless they could prove Denis had left the note, he couldn't be arrested.

Long after the officer had left and the pizza had

been eaten, at least by Reese, Sam tried to send him home.

"I'd rather stay. Here, on the couch," he hastily added when her eyes widened. "Seriously, Samantha, I don't like the idea of you being here alone. He clearly knows where you live. What's to stop him from coming back later tonight?"

"The door outside is locked."

"Yeah, but that didn't stop him from finding a way in before."

All it would take was for Denis to follow someone in who had a key, and they both knew it. She understood Reese was only being noble and, despite everything, she couldn't deny she liked having him near. Still, now that Denis knew about Reese, she was more worried than ever. What was to stop him from switching his threats from her to Reese? Or the other staff at Lifeline?

"Reese, go home. I need some time alone. Please, try to understand."

Reluctantly, he stood. "I don't understand, but I'll go. Here's my number." He hastily scribbled it on a notepad. "Call me, no matter what time. I'll come right over."

"I will." She forced a smile. "See you at work, Reese."

When he brushed a quick kiss across her lips, it was all she could do to keep her hands at her sides, when she really wanted to grab him and hold on tight. He left, closing the door softly behind him.

Samantha double-locked the door, then crossed

over to her kitchen table and sank into a chair, burying her face in her hands.

She'd lied when she'd told Reese she'd see him at work. First thing Monday morning, she was going to meet with Dr Jared O'Connor to request a reassignment.

She would miss flying, miss the responsibility of being a flight physician, but leaving would be the best thing for the rest of the Lifeline staff. Including Reese.

Especially Reese.

Monday morning, she hurried into Lifeline, anxious to see Jared before he was swamped with other problems or was called out on a pediatric flight.

When she burst into his office, though, she found him already deep in conversation with Reese. Her stomach clenched painfully. She didn't doubt Reese was filling Jared in on what a huge security risk she'd become.

"Samantha." Reese quickly stood. "We were just talking about you."

"Really? I wouldn't have guessed." Her sarcasm made him wince. "But if you don't mind, I'd rather discuss my personal problems with Jared—alone."

"Samantha, sit down. Please." Jared's voice held enough authority to make her drop into the chair next to Reese.

"Reese was filling me in on your ex-husband, and I must say I agree. Increasing security around here is the first order of business. Then we'll—"

"You don't need to do anything, Jared," Samantha

interrupted. "Except find someone to replace me. I'm formally requesting a reassignment."

"Request denied." Jared didn't even blink. "There's a private investigator I know, a guy by the name of Samuel Rafter. I think he can help us find your ex."

What was he talking about? "You can't deny my request."

"Sure I can." Jared smiled. "We've spent weeks training you, I can't replace you on a whim. Spring is coming and when the weather warms, the trauma calls will double. Besides, you're safer here, where we already have special security, than in another rotation."

"A whim?" Her voice sharpened. "A transfer is best for everyone's safety."

"And it's better for you to stay." Jared's tone brooked no arguments.

"Do you have a picture of Markowicz?" Reese wanted to know. "I think Rafter needs a picture."

Sam reached up to rub her aching temples. They weren't listening to her. "I don't have a picture. I didn't keep anything of our marriage." She looked up at Jared. "Please, think about this. I can stay long enough for you to train my replacement, then I'll leave."

"Last night you refused to run," Reese pointed out quietly. "Why don't you give Rafter a chance? He can do exactly what the police can't, follow Markowicz and catch him in the act. Once he's been arrested, you'll be safe."

Samantha could hardly imagine her life without

Denis looming in the background. The lure of possibly catching Denis in the act was one she couldn't resist. Heaven knew, she wanted her life back.

But if anything happened to the Lifeline crew, especially to Reese, she wasn't sure she could live with herself.

CHAPTER NINE

INDECISION warred within her. Finally, Sam nodded. "Okay. I won't run." At least, not yet, she silently amended. If the threats increased, all bets were off.

As the men discussed hiring Rafter and outlining the private investigator's duties, a ray of hope filtered into her heart. Maybe they were onto something. Reese was right. This guy could do things the police couldn't. Why hadn't she thought of a private investigator before now?

Because she'd been too busy running. The idea made her squirm. She'd worked so hard to get through medical school, to get accepted into an emergency medicine residency program. Now she was so close to graduating, to actually achieving success, that she'd chosen to keep running rather than to dig her heels in and fight.

"Since you don't have a picture, we'll need you to work with a police artist to do a sketch," Jared was saying.

"Is that necessary? I mean, Denis works at Beckley Pharmaceuticals. His identity isn't a secret." She paused. "At least, he did work there," she admitted. "But by now he could have a job with another company."

"Yeah, I think it's necessary. Shouldn't take long,

though.'' Jared glanced at his watch. "I'll arrange for it before you're scheduled to fly."

Since she knew she was on for the late shift, she nodded. "Anything else?"

"Just give Rafter the information he needs so he can do his job," Reese told her.

She shot him a narrow glance, not sure she was ready to forgive him for beating her to Jared. "I will."

Later that morning, she found herself once again in Jared's office, first creating a sketch of Denis then filling Rafter in on the awkward details of her personal life.

The sketch was eerily accurate. Reese had watched over the artist's shoulder as the drawing had taken shape. Then, to her relief, he and Jared left her alone to talk to Rafter.

She found it surprisingly easy to talk to the quiet private investigator. He didn't pass judgment or ooze with sympathy. He was an excellent listener. At least, until the end when she asked about his fees. Then he abruptly stood.

"You'll have to discuss the bill with Dr O'Connor," he told her hastily. "For now you've given me exactly what I need to work with."

Samantha stood, too. Darn Jared anyway. Was he really paying the bill or charging Lifeline for the services? Either way wasn't right. This was her personal problem, no one else's. "So you'll give me updates on what you find out?"

"As often as I can. Every few days to start, more

often if I find something worth bothering you about,'' he promised.

Samantha knew he would and the fact that Jared trusted him fueled her confidence. "Thanks."

Samantha returned to Lifeline a half hour prior to the start of her seven p.m. night shift. When she arrived, she sought out the printed version of the master schedule. Sure enough, Reese's name was written in alongside hers.

And not just for the upcoming shift. No, from the looks of things, he'd managed to manipulate his entire schedule to the point where it mirrored hers. Between Reese and Jared, she was beginning to feel her independence slip away.

She found Reese in the debriefing room, but didn't confront him right away. The offgoing shift was still there, updating the oncoming shift on their day's activities.

"Weather is supposed to turn foggy later," Nate, the day shift pilot, informed them. "Hope it holds off for a while."

"Me, too," Samantha agreed. The night shifts were long enough on their own, without adding flight delays. The minutes would crawl if they didn't get a chance to fly.

Ivan, the paramedic on duty with them, stifled a wide yawn. "I wouldn't mind a nap. Bethany is cutting teeth so I didn't get much sleep today."

Sam had seen pictures of Ivan's beautiful six-month-old daughter. She imagined it would be a challenge to sleep during the day with a baby in the house. "Did you work last night, too?"

Wearily, Ivan nodded. "Didn't get much sleep the day before either." His tone echoed with regret.

Their first flight call came in within the first hour of their shift. A single vehicle crash, car versus tree, made Sam suspect alcohol was involved. Sure enough, when they arrived, the driver of the car had been knocked out, the odor of alcohol strong on his breath. She performed a quick head-to-toe assessment while Ivan connected the guy to their equipment. Other than a huge bump on his head, the patient was surprisingly uninjured.

The police on the scene wanted to arrest him, but Sam overrode their wishes, insisting he go to Trinity for evaluation first. After a light debate, the officers agreed to meet them in the emergency department. She knew, from personal experience, that they would hang around until a decision was made to admit him or to discharge him. Only in this case, if their patient was discharged, he'd be taken straight to jail.

"How are things back there?" Reese asked as they headed toward Trinity.

"Fine. His head hurts too much for him to be a problem," Samantha replied. It wasn't unusual for patients to become combative, especially after sustaining a head injury under the influence of alcohol. But while her patient moaned frequently, he didn't thrash at the restraints.

They dropped him off at Trinity without mishap. The police arrived ten minutes later. Samantha and

Ivan completed their paperwork, then returned to the chopper.

They headed back to the Lifeline hangar to wait for another call. True to his word, Ivan stretched out on the sofa in the lounge, taking advantage of the downtime to close his eyes for some desperately needed sleep.

Samantha left him alone and returned to the debriefing room. She found Reese staring at the satellite monitor.

"How's the weather holding?" she asked.

"Not too good. Cloud ceiling has dropped, with intermittent patches of fog. If it drops any more, we won't fly."

Sam hoped the clouds would cooperate, then turned her attention from the monitor. "I noticed you managed to finesse your schedule to match mine. Didn't I tell you I don't need a baby-sitter?"

"This is work, Samantha. I'm paid to fly, just as you are." She almost laughed. As a resident, her pay was nearly nonexistent. "So what if my shifts are the same as yours?" His gaze darkened and he lowered his tone. "I prefer flying with you."

His simple statement made her breath catch in her throat. "I prefer flying with you, too, but that isn't the point."

"Then what is the point?" He stood, stepped closer then reached up to smooth away a strand of hair that had escaped from her braid. "You need to clarify it for me because I must be dense."

Her protest died at the brush of his fingertips on her cheek. While she knew he was the wrong man at the wrong time, she yearned for more. His strength. His caring.

His touch.

"I don't want anything to happen to you." She finally pushed the words past her constricted throat. "Denis might turn his anger toward you."

A feral grin tugged at his mouth. "Good. I hope he does just that."

"This isn't a joke," she said sharply, slapping her hand against his chest, encased in the navy blue flight suit.

His smile vanished and his hands settled on her waist, pulling her toward him. "I wasn't joking, Samantha. Why can't you trust me to protect you?"

"I trust you more than I've ever trusted any man." She didn't see any point in hiding the truth. "I don't want to see you hurt either."

"Your ex is too much of a coward to come after me." He eased her closer and she couldn't resist. His arms were strong and the urge to rest her head on his chest was, oh, so tempting.

Maybe he would protect her physically, but who would protect her heart? "Reese," she murmured, splaying her hands wide on his chest. "What am I going to do with you?"

"Kiss me." He brought her closer until she was pressed against him, and his mouth lowered to hers. This was no tentative brush of his lips against hers. No, this time he flat-out kissed her, his mouth parting her lips, urging her to respond.

She did. A thrill of excitement zipped along her nerves as his taste went to her head faster than champagne. She'd never felt so on edge, yet so protected at the same time. His hands stroked her back, smoothing over her bottom, pressing her closer.

His physical response was there, between them. She wanted to unzip his flight suit and explore the hard length of him. But he distracted her by tipping her head and trailing hot, sizzling kisses down the line of her jaw, pushing the fabric of her turtleneck sweater out of his way to press a kiss in the hollow of her throat.

Their pagers shrilled simultaneously. With reluctance, Reese lifted his head. Sam blinked, tried to focus.

"Multi-vehicle car crash," Sam said, reading the message on her pager. "Fifty miles north of here. I need to make sure Ivan is up."

"Don't. We're not responding to this call." Reese turned toward the phone.

"What?" Sam swung her gaze toward the monitor, to see if she'd missed something. "The cloud ceiling hasn't moved any lower. And the peds crew is out on a call."

"Paramedic base, we're in yellow flying conditions. We're not responding at this time." Reese's voice was calm as he gave the directive. "You might want to contact the peds crew to let them know the change in conditions here. They might want to stay put for a while."

"Reese, I don't want to fly in poor conditions any more than you do, but are you sure there isn't a way to respond?" The aborted flight was still fresh in her mind, but it wasn't even snowing, just a low cloud ceiling. "Those people need help. A few minutes ago you said if the ceiling drops lower, we won't fly. Well it hasn't dropped lower, it's the same." She could barely keep the frustration in her voice. "I think we should respond to this call."

"No. You don't understand the weather conditions like a pilot does." His calm voice didn't seem to betray any hint of regret, which only ticked her off.

"You're the one who changed his tune," she argued. "So don't tell me I don't understand. If this is your attitude, maybe I'd be better off flying with Nate or one of the other pilots."

Reese's dark brown eyes turned black. "You don't know the risks. I do. The weather can change in a heartbeat. Have you read the detailed crash reports after a fatality? Especially when one of the crew members that died happened to be the woman you loved?"

The horror in his gaze caught her by the throat. Reese had always seemed cool and in control. But he wasn't cool now. "No," she whispered.

"Well, I have. It isn't pretty." Reese jammed his hands into the pockets of his flight suit. He hunched his shoulders, as if embarrassed by his outburst. Calmer now, he continued, "The wind is coming in from the north, right over the lake. The crash scene is also fifty miles to the north. When the warmer air over the lake hits the cold north wind, the fog will get worse. Remember the other night, when we were suddenly in the middle of a snowstorm? The lake makes the weather unpredictable. That's why I turned down the flight."

"Oh." She felt small, petty for arguing with him about something she knew so little about. Clearly Reese was the best one to make the decision either way. "You're right. As the pilot, you should be the one making the call."

"Not necessarily." Reese rubbed his eyes, then leaned his hips against the edge of the desk. "Some pilots would fly in this weather. I'm just not one of them. But you should have the right to decide for yourself, too. Each crew member should."

Sam didn't quite know what to say to that. But she remembered the sad look in his eyes a few days ago and, when combined with his most recent comments, the truth clicked. "Who was she?" she asked.

His head snapped up. "What do you mean?"

"The woman you loved and lost to a crash." The signs were so clear now that she knew to look for them. Everyone joked about Reese peering over Mitch's shoulder, how he took flying safety so seriously. But none of them had understood why. If there had been any rumors about Reese's past, she hadn't heard them.

He was silent for so long she thought he wasn't going to answer. "Valerie. We were engaged to be married. My best friend, Greg Hasking, was the pilot. The paramedic on board was Jim Wahlen, a guy who left behind a wife and two kids."

Dear God. Sorrow washed over her. Samantha couldn't imagine how the paramedic's widow must have felt, losing her husband so young. And Reese. How had he survived, losing two people so close to him? "They all died?"

Reese slowly nodded. "They were flying on a transport and got caught in a snowstorm in the mountains of Colorado. I— They shouldn't have been flying. The weather was too risky."

"I'm sorry, Reese." She longed to comfort him, to soothe his pain. "I'm so sorry for your loss."

He shrugged lightly. "Valerie knew the risks and she loved to fly. I just wish I had been there, like I was supposed to be. I'd switched shifts with Greg."

She winced, knowing how that fact would have only added to Reese's guilt. "It's not your fault."

"I should have been there." His flat tone betrayed the depth of his grief.

Sam ached for him, for what he'd lost. For the paramedic's wife and children. "You're here now. And it's selfish of me, but I'm glad." She crossed over to him, placed a hesitant hand on his arm. "I'm very glad, Reese."

"Samantha." His voice turned husky when she slid her hand up and wrapped her arms around his neck to pull him toward her in a gesture meant to give comfort. He dipped his head to rest on her shoulder, his arms loose around her waist. "I'm glad, too," he whispered against her temple.

Her heart soared and she blinked away unexpected tears. She threaded her hands through his hair, enjoying the silky texture against her fingertips.

His grip tightened at her waist and he turned his face into her neck. "God, you smell so good. Like Christmas every day."

She smiled, tipping her head to allow him better

access, cursing winter and the need for warm clothes. She clutched at his shoulders.

He groaned low in his throat and lifted his head, taking several gulping breaths. "We'd better stop. I'm not sure how much of this I can take."

"Maybe I don't want to stop." Sam bravely met his gaze.

His eyes widened in a way that would have been comic if she hadn't wanted him so badly. "There's no rush, Samantha. You aren't ready for a relationship, remember?"

"And you pointed out how it was already too late," she reminded him right back. Reaching up, she cupped his cheek in her hand. "I care about you, Reese. You're the first man in years to tempt me into throwing caution to the wind."

He kissed her, clutching her close and showing the effect her words had on him. "God, Samantha. I want you to be sure," he said finally, lifting his head and looking directly into her eyes. "Your career is important to you and boards are only a few short months away. We can wait until after you've taken them, if you want. For now I'm content to simply hold you."

The blazing hunger in his gaze was a far cry from his chaste words and Samantha was touched by his willingness to wait. Had she ever met a man who'd put her needs first? Medical school had been competitive, each student vying for the best grades to ensure the best residency match. When she'd married Denis, and he hadn't made the final cut, things had gone from competitive to controlling.

Yet here was Reese, hard with desire but willing

to do whatever was better for her. Not controlling her, not trying to compete with her career, but supporting her decisions, whatever they might be.

"I'm sure, Reese." She toyed with the zipper on his flight suit. "I've never felt this way before, ever. I want you."

"Oh, man, what a thing to say when we have a long shift ahead of us." Reese laughed and groaned at the same time. He pressed a kiss to the top of her head. "You're dangerous, woman, you know that?"

"We're alone here." She tugged his zipper down a few inches, the sound loud in the otherwise silent room. "The peds crew is on their way to Michigan then back to Children's Memorial, so they won't be back for hours. Ivan's dead to the world and your pilot's sleeping room has a door with a lock on it."

She'd noticed the room right away the first time she'd come to Lifeline. At the time she'd thought it odd that the physicians didn't have a similar space to sleep, and Jared had explained how the residents were transient but the pilots were assigned on a permanent basis. Right now she didn't much care whose room it was. Privacy was only a few steps away.

"I have to keep an eye on the weather," Reese murmured, his voice hitching as she tugged his zipper lower still. His hands came up to capture her wrists.

"Do you think the fog is going to dissipate that quickly?" she asked, pressing closer.

"No." In that moment she knew she'd won. Reese swung her into his arms and stalked toward the small pilot's sleeping room. Once inside, he kicked the door closed behind him.

She tensed, half expecting him to toss her on the bed, but instead he set her gently on her feet. "There's time to change your mind," he offered.

The zipper on the front of his flight suit gave away beneath the pressure of her fingers. "I won't."

He slowly undressed her, as if she were fragile instead of flesh and blood. "I don't want to scare you. Did he...hurt you?"

"No. Only with words, not the way you're thinking." She didn't want the ugliness of her past to mar this moment between them. "I won't break." Frustrated, she shoved the navy blue fabric from his broad shoulders, wishing he would do the same to her. His chest wasn't bare beneath his flight suit; he wore a thin long-sleeved T-shirt as protection from the cold.

While she knew it would be foolish to fly in subzero temperatures without being prepared for a long flight, she resented the cumbersome layers now. "I want to see you."

"Not half as badly as I want to see you."

Because it was quicker, if less romantic, they each dealt with their own clothes. Reese laughed when her boots got stuck in the leg openings of her flight suit in her haste to get them off.

The sound of his deep, husky laugh made her smile. Pleased to be at least partly responsible, she shot him a shy glance.

"You have a great laugh, Reese. I'd like to hear it more often."

He dropped his own boots with a thud. "You will."

When she was completely naked, his gaze hungrily roved over her. "You're so beautiful, Samantha."

She melted into his open arms. They eased onto the bed, taking time to savor the experience. Not once did he try to control her. Rather, he allowed her to lead the way, although she could see it wasn't easy. The corded tendons in his neck and the bunching muscles in his arms betrayed the depth of his restraint. His ability to maintain a semblance of self-control as she explored every inch of him only made her want him more.

They shared, touch for touch, kiss for kiss, until at last he found a condom and, after sheathing himself, slid deep. Even then he didn't take over.

"Tell me what you want, Samantha." His voice, gritty with need, tickled her ear. "Hard and fast or slow and deep. Tell me what you want."

"You." She gasped and clutched at him when he thrust again. "All I want is you."

"You have me." Was it a threat or a promise? She didn't know, couldn't think.

All too soon desire melted into hot need, cresting into searing pleasure. Until she lay replete in his arms.

Overcome with tenderness and awe, she blinked away sudden tears. So *this* was how love was supposed to feel.

Reese stared at the ceiling, Samantha cradled against his chest, loath to move. Over the long hours of the night he'd checked the radar frequently, updating the paramedic base on the nasty turn of the weather before crawling back into his warm bed and Samantha's waiting arms. Now dawn was only a short hour away. They needed to get up soon, but he didn't want to disturb Samantha.

He'd broken his rule by getting involved with her. Although he'd tried to hold her off until after she'd graduated, he hadn't possessed the willpower to hold out against her.

Idly, he smoothed a hand over her silky skin. These hours they'd shared had been the best he'd spent in months. Not just the intense pleasure, but the closeness. The way she'd giggled when he'd got dressed, *sans* underwear and boots, to creep into the control room, update the base, then sneak back into bed again.

Thank God Ivan had needed his sleep or he might have wandered in to find them. Still could, in fact, if he happened to get up early. He glanced at his watch. The peds crew was due in soon, unless they chose to wait out the weather at Children's Memorial. Pressing a kiss onto Sam's bare shoulder, he slowly drew away, inch by inch.

This time he dressed properly, knowing there would be no crawling back to bed. At least, not until they were home. Would Samantha allow him in her apartment? Or was this single magical night the only one they'd share?

"Samantha, honey, you'd better get up." He gently shook her shoulder once he was safely dressed. "I'll be in the debriefing room. You need to get dressed."

"Hmm." She smiled at him, her beautiful smoky gray eyes heavy-lidded with sleep. "Okay."

He grinned as he headed into the debriefing room.

Damn, he could get used to waking up with Samantha in his arms. The weather had turned into a storm early this morning, the wind howling and the swirling snow dropping visibility to mere inches. The storm had been unexpected and, needless to say, they wouldn't be flying any time in the next few hours.

After updating the paramedic base and verifying that the Lifeline peds crew would leave the chopper at Children's Memorial and get a taxi back, he logged onto his e-mail. The first item to capture his attention was an alert from Pilots Incorporated, the voluntary organization of helicopter rescue pilots sharing medical air flight information across the country.

"Crash alert. Chicago's Air Angel suffered a fatal helicopter crash at 0200 hours this morning. Fatalities included the entire crew, pilot, flight nurse and flight physician. Our prayers go out to the crew's family and friends."

Stunned, Reese stared at the message. There were bound to be other factors surrounding the crash, but one thing was for sure. Chicago's weather often mirrored theirs.

The pilot had crashed flying in weather Reese had refused to fly in.

CHAPTER TEN

REESE quickly shut down his e-mail when Samantha entered the debriefing room. A part of him wanted to protect her from the horror of the crash while the logical portion of his brain insisted she was better off knowing the risks.

"You didn't make any coffee?" Sam's voice echoed with disappointment.

"Sorry. I don't drink coffee." He double-clicked on the e-mail icon and the crash message bloomed on the screen. With another couple of keystrokes he printed out the message. He heard running water as she prepared to brew a fresh pot. "I have some bad news here."

"Bad news?" She hurried back into the debriefing room. "Denis?"

"No, not that." He could have kicked himself for reminding her. Although he wasn't sure the crash news was any better. He handed her the copy of his e-mail message. "Better sit down before reading this."

"Oh, no." Her eyes drank in the message, then lifted to meet his. "Reese, this is awful. Chicago is only about seventy miles away."

"I know." He sat heavily in his seat beside the satellite monitor.

"But this could have been us." Agitated now, she

leapt to her feet. She ran a hand through her hair, left down instead of braided after their night together, and paced the short length of the room. "I was insisting we fly to the crash scene last night. If we had gone, we could have crashed. Just like this."

Reese couldn't deny the grim truth. "There may be other mitigating factors we're not aware of," he pointed out. "The FAA will do a thorough investigation before making a final determination."

"A final determination of what?" Ivan asked, scratching his chin as he entered the room. "Samantha, you're a doll for making coffee."

"On the cause of the crash." Reese knew Ivan had been flying long enough to know the risks.

Ivan's expression turned somber. "Who crashed?"

"Air Angel." Reese handed him the message. "Last night at 0200."

"What were the flying conditions?" Ivan asked as his gaze flickered over the e-mail.

"Patches of fog but a cold wind coming in from the north." Reese filled him in on the events of last night, including the decision to keep one chopper at Children's Memorial rather than risk a return flight. "You were sleeping so soundly we didn't wake you."

"Thanks." His white teeth flashed in a grin. "My wife will appreciate your thoughtfulness. I can help out with Bethany today, rather than trying to sleep in snatches."

Reese nodded, not about to mention how he and Samantha had benefited from Ivan's exhaustion. "Is Jared in yet?"

Ivan shook his head. "No, I think he's going to be late today. Shelly has her first doctor's appointment this morning." When Reese's eyes widened in alarm, the paramedic hastened to reassure him. "Haven't you heard? She's pregnant."

His expression cleared. "No, I hadn't heard. I'm happy for them, though."

"Shelly, the peds flight nurse?" Samantha halted her pacing to turn and glance at them. "I knew she married Jared a few months ago and that they both still fly. Now she's pregnant?"

Clearly, the news of the fatal crash was still too fresh and painful. "Knowing Jared, he won't allow Shelly to keep flying once she's further along." Reese tried to console her.

"Yeah, but you're assuming Shelly will listen," Ivan pointed out dryly.

Since Reese already knew how stubborn Flight Nurse Shelly O'Connor could be, he held his tongue. "Samantha, calm down. Lifeline has an excellent twenty-year crash-free history. Safety is our prime concern."

"I know." She tried to smile, but failed miserably. "At least, I do now. I'm glad you insisted on remaining grounded last night."

Reese rubbed his hands over his face and wished he'd acquired a taste for coffee. He could use the kick of caffeine to help dissolve the fog in his brain. The decision he'd made had been gut instinct more than anything. He could have just as easily agreed to fly. He'd been honest with Samantha last night, the weather could always change without warning. The day they'd tried to fly to Two Rivers, only to head back because of the weather, was proof of how even the best pilot could find himself facing poor flying conditions.

The truth was difficult to deny. Anyone could crash. He could lose Samantha, the same way he'd lost Valerie.

Long after Ivan had gone home, Reese buried his head in paperwork he'd neglected while waiting for Jared. He had a plan that he needed Jared's approval to implement.

Samantha had given him a strange look when he'd told her he needed to work late today. He knew he was treating her badly, especially after the night they'd shared, but the news of the crash had shaken him more than he'd wanted to admit. Putting some distance between him and Samantha seemed prudent.

He heard voices in the hallway outside the debriefing room and wondered if Jared had finally arrived. Piling the reports in a neat stack, he grabbed his proposal and pushed away from the desk.

The voices came from Jared's office. He paused outside the partially open door, trying to figure out who was in there. In a heartbeat he recognized Samantha's husky voice.

"What's your plan?" Jared asked.

"My only real plan for the moment is to ace my boards," Reese heard her respond. "But after that I was thinking of moving to the West Coast, to the San Diego area. My parents still live there, even though my siblings are scattered across the country."

Reese felt a sharp pain in his abdomen, as if he'd been punched. Samantha planned to move after graduation? She hadn't mentioned those plans to him.

"Let me know. I'd be happy to write you a glowing letter of recommendation," Jared was saying. "In the meantime, I'll keep you posted on whatever information Rafter comes up with."

"Thanks. I appreciate it."

Reese steadied himself on the door frame, Samantha's words swirling around in his head. When he sensed their conversation was over, he pulled himself together, rapped his knuckle against the wood and poked his head through the doorway. "Jared? Do you have a minute?"

"Sure." Jared and Samantha stood up. "Talk to you later, Samantha."

She nodded and smiled at Reese, an unspoken question in her gaze. "See you both later."

He knew she wanted to know if she'd see him sooner rather than later, but Reese couldn't bring himself to answer. Neither did he stop her from leaving, much as he wanted to. Even though her future plans had shaken him, he knew Markowicz was still out there. He trusted Rafter, but the need to follow Samantha home was strong.

He forced himself to let her go.

"What's on your mind, Reese?" Jared asked, settling in behind his desk.

"A team approach to flying." He handed Jared his proposal before sitting across from him. "Did you hear about the Air Angel crash last night?"

Jared frowned. "No."

Reese quickly filled him in. "I'm a cautious pilot by nature, but not every pilot sees weather conditions exactly the same way. With each takeoff, safety measures will only go so far. You know as well as I do there are many factors outside our control."

"I'm with you so far," Jared commented.

"I'm proposing that each team member has the right to decide if they feel comfortable flying in dicey weather conditions. If even one person has reservations, the flight is called off. The captain doesn't have veto rights, insisting it's safe to fly."

"Interesting proposal," Jared murmured, skimming the information Reese had handed him. "Have any other air transport companies initiated a similar policy?"

"Not that I'm aware of." Reese couldn't lie. "In fact, companies that are in it for profit will push the limit on flying conditions. Air Angel just happens to be a commercial company."

Jared thoughtfully nodded. "We're lucky to be subsidized by the area hospitals and the state, allowing us to remain nonprofit status." He tapped the proposal. "I like this, Reese. I say we implement your plan immediately. We'll track the flight refusals and see how it goes."

Relief loosened the tight bands around his chest. "Thanks, Jared. I appreciate your support."

"I have as much invested in this program as you do," Jared pointed out. His gaze dropped to the proposal. "In some ways, more than you do."

It didn't take a genius to figure out Jared was thinking about his wife and unborn child. "I know." He cleared his throat. "I take it there's no news from Rafter yet?"

Jared shook his head. "Not yet. He's dug into Markowicz's background, though, and has staked out his condo. I'm sure we'll hear something soon. At least, when he makes a move toward Samantha, we'll know."

Guilt flooded Reese. He should have followed her home. "Keep me posted, too."

If Jared thought his request was strange, he didn't mention it. "I will. Get some sleep."

Reese drove home, knowing sleep would be a long time coming. He actually pulled into the parking space next to Samantha's before realizing what he'd done. With a muttered curse he threw his truck in Reverse and headed home.

Inside, he couldn't dredge up his usually insatiable appetite. His team approach to flying might have saved Valerie, but not if she'd been willing to go. The memory of Valerie didn't hurt the way it used to. Samantha's words came floating back to him. He should have followed his instincts and stayed far away from her. The time they would have together could be measured in days, maybe months, before she'd leave.

Pain tightened his throat as realization dawned. Losing Samantha would be far worse than when he'd lost Valerie. Because Valerie hadn't had a choice. He'd known she'd loved him.

He didn't have Samantha's love, although he knew she cared for him. Still, when she left, she'd simply walk away.

* * *

Samantha should have been exhausted, but she couldn't sleep. Not that sleeping in the bright light of daytime had ever been easy. She'd struggled when other residents she knew could drop off no matter what time of the day it was.

But the problem right now was Reese. The night they'd shared had been wonderful. Better than wonderful. But in the morning his whole attitude had changed.

She couldn't really blame him. News of the Air Angel crash was enough to ruin anyone's mood. But she couldn't help but wonder about the woman Reese had loved. The woman he'd asked to marry him. To be jealous of a dead woman was utterly foolish, but her heart twisted painfully anyway.

Had he felt guilty for making love with her? Reese had been a willing participant during the night, the sight of him, sneaking from their bed, pulling his flight suit over his naked body and tiptoeing out to check the satellite monitor still making her smile.

Slowly, her smile faded. No, Reese's demeanor hadn't changed until this morning, when he'd read the news of the crash. Obviously, he was still torn up inside over losing his fiancée. What had she been like, this woman who still had a hold on Reese's heart? She tossed her arm over her eyes, trying to block out the endless questions. What did it matter what the woman had been like? Reese wasn't in Colorado anymore. He was here at Lifeline now.

But had he left his heart behind, buried with a woman who'd died in the mountains? She didn't know.

How ironic that the first man she'd grown to love and trust in the years since she'd mistaken Denis's companionship for love wasn't in a position to return those feelings in kind.

A clunk outside her bedroom window woke her out of a sound sleep. Groggily, she blinked, trying to read the luminous numbers on her clock. Six in the evening. She'd only managed to sleep for a few hours.

Sliding her feet into slippers, Samantha crossed the room. With a frown she peered through the window. Had she heard something, or had it been her imagination? Since finding her smashed car battery, she tended to suspect Denis lurking around every corner.

The shrill ringing of her phone drew her attention and she immediately stepped away from the window. The moment she moved a loud crash burst from behind her. She instinctively screamed and threw herself to the floor.

She heard a shout followed by a yell somewhere outside. Samantha raised her head from the floor, glancing around in fear. Her bedroom window was broken, a gaping hole in the center surrounded by jagged glass. The opening wasn't large enough for a person, she noted in relief. Had Denis struck again?

Her phone was still ringing, so she jumped to her feet and dashed into the kitchen. "Hello?"

Too late. The mystery person on the other end of the line had hung up. Shivering with the cold February air flowing freely through the broken window, she found her Lifeline jacket and slipped it on over her flannel sweats. Shaking, she tried to decide what to do first. Call the police? Call to have her broken window repaired? Take care of the broken glass splattered around her room?

Edging down the hall, she stood in the doorway of her bedroom. Lying in the center of her bed was a large, heavy brick. Wrapped around the brick was some sort of brown paper. Even from this distance she could see a message written on the note, addressed to her.

She didn't want to read it, knowing the note would be more of the same. *Come home, where you belong.* Turning from the mess in her room, she returned to the kitchen. Seeing the brick had helped her make a decision. Police first, then repair the window.

She'd already called the police when she heard more noise from outside. A car engine, then the slam of a car door. She tensed. Had Denis come back?

"Samantha!" She heard someone shout her name a moment before there was pounding on her apartment door. "Are you all right? Open up."

"Reese?" She peered through the peephole, surprised and very relieved to see him standing there. She opened the door. "What are you doing here?"

"Are you all right?" He came forward and cupped her face in his hands, brushing his thumbs over her cheeks. "Rafter called me when you didn't answer your phone, telling me he pegged Markowicz outside your building."

The wild look in his eye belayed her fear. "I'm fine. But my window isn't."

"I thought it was cold in here." Reese pressed his mouth against hers in a brief, hard kiss. Then he glanced around the apartment. "What happened?"

"A noise outside woke me up." His kiss rattled her brains and she frowned in concentration. "I...uh, got up and went over to the window to see if anyone was out there. Then my phone started to ring, so I stepped away to answer it. I heard a crash and hit the floor." She was embarrassed at her reaction, cowering in fear instead of facing the danger head-on. "Someone hurled a brick through my window."

"Someone? Markowicz?" Reese's hands tightened on her arms. "Dammit, he could have hit you. The next time you hear a noise, don't go anywhere near a window!"

"I won't." The closeness of her near miss, along with the cold air, made her teeth chatter.

"Did you call the police?"

She nodded. "They're on their way."

Reese led her over to the sofa, urging her to sit. "Stay here. I'll check out the damage."

Sam clasped her hands together to stop them from trembling. "I know Denis is probably long gone, but I'll need the police report to pay for the broken window."

He disappeared down the hall toward her bedroom. Samantha sat for a moment, then realized she was doing it again, letting others take control of her life. Jumping to her feet, she followed him.

"Stay back." His voice was harsh. "You'll cut yourself. There's glass everywhere."

Since her bare feet felt like twin blocks of ice, she

knew she wouldn't feel a sharp edge until it was too late. She hovered in the doorway, surveying the mess in her room. "How am I going to get the glass out of the carpet?"

Reese's normally calm features reflected his seething anger. "I don't know, but we can't touch anything the cops may be able to use as evidence. I hope Rafter managed to get some evidence, too." He turned away from the window. "Tell me what you need so I can get it for you."

Samantha directed him to where her shoes, socks, jeans and sweaters were located. After their closeness the night before, there was no reason for her face to burn as he went through her drawers, pulling out the items she'd requested, including clean underwear. Once he'd retrieved her things she took them gratefully and disappeared into the bathroom to change.

She felt more in control when she emerged, fully dressed, a few minutes later. The police arrived fast, the broken window rating a higher threat than her earlier note. While she answered their questions, she noticed Reese talking on his cell phone.

"Was that Rafter?" she asked, breaking away from the police officer's questions.

Reese nodded. "Yeah. I called and asked him to come over. He's on his way. He almost had his hands on Markowicz, but the guy managed to slip away."

She couldn't hide the sharp disappointment. So close, they had been so close to nailing Denis in the act. Sam forced herself to remain calm. "Next time, I guess."

"Damn. There shouldn't have to be a next time."

Reese's frustration mirrored hers. He'd raked his hands through his hair so many times the strands stood on end, sticking out of his head at odd angles. She suspected he'd recently woken from sleep himself. "I thought Rafter was better than this. I can't believe he let the jerk get away."

Samantha felt the same way, although she knew Denis was craftier than most people thought. Underestimating him was only too easy. She'd married him thinking he was a great guy, with similar goals and desires to hers.

She'd been wrong. Right now she was finding out just how wrong she'd been about him.

The police combed her apartment, taking photographs of the mess in her bedroom and dusting for prints on the wall surrounding the outside of her window and on the brick itself. After a few minutes, her buzzer sounded.

Hesitantly, she crossed the room. "Yes?"

"It's Rafter."

"Come on in." She pushed the button to release the outside lock, then opened her apartment door.

Rafter didn't look upset to have lost his man. In fact, a broad grin creased his features. In his hands he held several photographs.

"We got him." He displayed the photos on her kitchen table. "I have a digital camera and downloaded these a few minutes ago."

Reese crossed over to take a look. Samantha caught her breath. The pictures were amazingly clear. Rafter had caught a clear photo of Denis outside her window, holding what looked like the brick in his hand.

"Great." Reese clapped a hand on Rafter's shoulder. "I admit I couldn't believe you'd allowed him to escape."

"The pictures had to come first or, trust me, I would have had him. I honestly didn't even see the brick in his hand at first. I didn't know he'd planned to chuck it through her window until I saw the swing of his arm. But at least we have the evidence needed for the police to arrest him."

Samantha lifted her gaze from the eerie photos. The officer who'd questioned her entered the room, the pictures drawing his attention.

"Markowicz is in clear violation of his restraining order and, more, this shows his attempted assault." The officer picked up the picture of Denis holding the brick, mere seconds before he'd launched it through her window. "I'll send out the team to stake out his house, authorizing his arrest."

Samantha pressed a shaking hand over her heart. It was over. Denis would be arrested soon and the nightmare would be over.

CHAPTER ELEVEN

REESE stared at the window he'd boarded up in Samantha's room. Like winter wasn't dark enough, he thought ruefully. With the plywood nailed across the opening, there would be no light streaming in. Raking a hand through his hair, he stepped back. The police had finally left and so had Rafter. The PI still had a guy staking out Samantha's building, but he seriously doubted that Markowicz would show. He'd be too busy getting arrested.

Still, he didn't like leaving Samantha here alone. But how to convince her to move in temporarily with him? After their stilted conversation earlier this morning, he knew he'd botched things badly. He was probably the last guy on earth, other than that slime Markowicz, she wanted to spend time with.

"I suppose you're hungry." Samantha entered the room, surveying his handiwork. "Thanks for fixing my window."

If only he could fix more than the stupid window. "No problem. It's the least I can do."

She raised a brow. "Why is that? My broken window is hardly your problem."

He sighed, met her gaze. "I guess it's my way of apologizing for the way I acted this morning."

With a shrug she glanced away. "It's all right. I

can only imagine the horrible memories you must have of the crash."

It wasn't just the crash, but he couldn't bring himself to bring up the subject of her plans to move to San Diego after graduation. Not her fault that he'd fallen in love with her. He hadn't ever expected to feel this much for any woman ever again. "I didn't get the chance to tell you how much last night meant to me."

Her gaze shot to his. "I thought you were having second thoughts."

Slowly, he shook his head. "No. You've made me feel alive, Samantha. I would never regret our time together." No matter how short that time might be.

A hopeful smile bloomed on her face. "I'm glad."

"Will you come back to my place? We can pick up something to eat on the way." He held his breath, prepared for her refusal.

"I have to work in the morning," she hedged. Then she shook her head. "And since you've switched your schedule to match mine, so do you."

"I know. I'm asking you to stay with me. All night." He'd missed her when he'd come home. His bed had been glaringly lonely without her snuggled up beside him.

For a long moment she stared at him. "Reese, I don't need protecting anymore. For all we know, the police have already arrested Denis."

He nodded. He wanted to touch her, to pull her into his arms. He forced himself to keep his hands at his sides. "I know. I'm not asking you to stay with me because of Markowicz. I'm asking because I want to spend time with you.''

''All night?'' Samantha wryly asked, one brow raised questioningly.

He swallowed hard, disappointment searing his chest. ''Only to talk, if that's what you want.''

She laughed. ''Oh, Reese, the look on your face.''

Was she teasing him? A smile creased his lips and he strove to appear innocent. ''What? I would spend the time talking, if that's what you wanted.''

''But that's not what you want, is it?''

No. Lord above, he craved much more than that. But he wouldn't rush her, or push her into anything more than she was willing to give. ''What I want isn't important.''

She crossed the room and laid a hand on his chest. He nearly gasped as the heat of it burned through the fabric of his T-shirt. ''It is to me.''

His heart raced at her implication. ''I— Damn, woman. Don't say stuff like that to me.''

''Why not? I mean it, Reese.''

He clenched his hands into fists. Jumping her bones here in her room where there would still be shards of glass lying around was not a part of the plan. He could hang on for a few more minutes. Maybe. ''Pack a bag, Samantha. Please. And don't forget your flight suit.''

Samantha couldn't remember ever sleeping better than she had in Reese's arms. The only disappointment had come when Reese called Rafter after they'd gotten up for work that morning. So far the police hadn't arrested Denis because he hadn't gone home.

She told herself it was only a matter of time. Denis couldn't hide forever. Reese offered to drive them to work and, since she'd be coming back with him at the end of their shift, it seemed ridiculous to refuse. Still, she didn't like the idea of the two of them showing up in the same car together. The staff at Lifeline was small and gossip spread quickly.

"I'd rather take my own car." Samantha braced herself for an argument.

Reese's frown told her he didn't like her decision, but he didn't try to talk her out of it either. "All right. But at least let me drive you over there."

Sam relaxed. She knew Reese wasn't like Denis, needing to control her every move. The way he gave in gracefully to her wishes warmed her heart. Maybe there was something to this relationship thing after all.

The sky was clear but the wind was sharp as they headed inside the hangar a little later. Andrew was the paramedic on duty with her again today. Luckily he didn't seem to notice that she and Reese arrived at close to the same time.

Although she knew it was foolish, she didn't want to announce her relationship with Reese to the whole world. Especially since she didn't know if he was truly over Valerie.

The night shift gave their debriefing, anxious to leave and go home. Less than an hour later their first call came in.

"Scene call. Some guy fell through the ice on Lake Minooka while ice fishing."

"Did they get him out?" she asked.

"Not yet."

"Let's get there before they do."

The three of them grabbed their helmets and dashed for the chopper. Lake Minooka was a good fifteen-minute flight away, and in cases of severe hypothermia every second counted.

Samantha nervously clutched the roll bar and held her breath when Reese lifted the chopper off the ground. She hadn't expected to feel so nervous about flying. It wasn't as if she didn't trust Reese, because she did. Still, several minutes went by before she could pry her fingers off the roll bar.

"Hey, Doc. You okay?" Andrew asked, concern in his gaze.

"Something wrong, Samantha?" Reese immediately asked from the pilot's seat, picking up on Andrew's observation.

"Nothing's wrong. I'm fine." Samantha maintained an even tone. "Honest. Just get us to the scene, Reese, as quickly as possible."

"Roger."

The chopper banked and Samantha was relieved when her initial nervousness faded. How had Reese managed to get into the cockpit again after Valerie had crashed? Flying again after something like that was true bravery.

"We're coming up on Lake Minooka, but we need to find a place to land that's not too close to the lake." Reese's voice flowed through her headset.

She frowned. "I don't understand. Why can't we get close to the lake?"

"The noise and wind speed of the blades could break up the rest of the ice," Andrew explained. "If the rescue crew are still on the ice, they'd all fall in."

Samantha peered out her window. "How much room do you need, Reese? There's a road about a hundred yards from the lake to the south. If there was a way to block off the traffic, would that work?"

"I see it and, yes, the location is perfect. I'll radio the base."

They wasted precious minutes as they relayed the information to the officials at the scene. Reese finally landed the chopper. Andrew and Samantha didn't waste any time. They needed to cross the distance between the helicopter and the lake.

They were both breathing heavily when they pulled up at the group of rescue workers gathered around the lake. "Did you get him out?" Sam asked.

"Yeah, but he doesn't have a pulse. The firefighters are working on him now."

Sam elbowed her way to the patient's side. "How long was he under?" she asked.

"Ten minutes. The icy water might have worked in our favor, though."

With a nod she indicated she understood. The body required less oxygen when submerged in icy water. But ten minutes was still a very long time.

"Hey, I think I feel a pulse."

Samantha placed her fingers along the carotid artery as well. "I do, too."

"Let's get some meds into him before we lose it again."

She helped the firefighters while Andrew prepared the gurney. The patient's heart rate had returned, but the rhythm was hardly regular.

"Lidocaine first. And make sure we have the defibrillator charged up. We could lose his rhythm any moment."

Thankfully, the firefighters had started an IV. "Andrew, do you have the warmer on?"

"You bet." He finished switching over all the equipment, including the IV. On the count of three they lifted the patient and swung him onto the cart.

"Let's go." Samantha took a deep breath, preparing for the long hike to the chopper.

"Here, use this ambulance." One of the firefighters gestured to the waiting vehicle. "You'll get over there much faster. The guy has to weigh at least ninety kilos."

"Thanks." Samantha gratefully accepted his offer.

They reached the helicopter in record time. Reese had the blades whirling, ready to go.

She and Andrew loaded the patient through the hatch. Andrew gestured for her to follow the patient inside, then closed the door after her.

When Andrew was settled in beside her, she switched on her mike. "We're good to go back here, Reese."

"Roger. Base, we're preparing for liftoff."

Samantha busied herself with hooking up the warming blanket and spreading it out to cover their patient. Then she checked the medication while

Andrew began filling out the paperwork. "I'm losing his rhythm here," she warned. "He's having mega-PVCs. I'm giving another bolus of lidocaine and increasing the drip."

"Got it." Andrew jotted down the notations, then reached over to power up the defibrillator. "Let me know if you want to cardiovert."

"I will." Samantha gave the medication, then watched the effects on the monitor. "We still have a pulse, and a borderline stable blood pressure. Let's wait to see what the meds can do."

"Is everything all right back there?" Reese asked. "Do you need me to divert our course?"

"Negative. We're holding our own. At least for the moment." Samantha wondered how Reese seemed able to read every inflection of her tone. Although he was seated in the cockpit, she always felt as if he were right beside her.

There was no time to be afraid of flying as they neared Trinity Medical Center. "Reese, radio ahead and tell them I need a hot unload."

"Will do." She barely listened as Reese did as she'd asked. "ETA in roughly five minutes."

"Come on, buddy, hang on," she murmured, giving her patient another bolus of lidocaine. She gave a little extra, thinking they might have underestimated the patient's weight. For all they knew, he could be closer to 110 kg.

"Getting ready to land," Reese informed them.

The minutes had never gone so fast. "We're ready."

As soon as Reese landed, Andrew jumped out to

release the hatch. Between them they pulled out their patient and set him down. The ED staff were waiting as requested on the helipad.

"Core temp is still barely 30 degrees centigrade. And he's still having lots of PVCs," Samantha shouted as they wheeled him inside.

"Thank heavens you guys got there when you did, or he wouldn't have had any chance at all," one of the ED nurses commented.

Samantha wordlessly agreed. They took their patient into the closest trauma bay and continued to work on him while another nurse called up to the ICU. Samantha and Andrew stepped aside. Their role in saving this ice fisherman's life was over, but he wasn't out of the woods yet.

But the nurse had been right. Flying was actually safer than ground transport. Besides, without Lifeline, this guy wouldn't have had a chance to live.

"Everything go okay?" Reese asked, once they'd climbed back on board.

"Yeah, for now. He's in good hands," Samantha told him.

"I need to refuel before heading back to the hangar."

"Sounds good."

The extra trip added close to twenty minutes before they arrived back at Lifeline. Inside the debriefing room and out of Andrew's earshot, Reese caught Samantha's arm. "Are you really all right?" he asked in a low tone.

"I'm fine." She tried to shrug, but Reese only

tightened his grip and she knew her casual tone hadn't fooled him. "For a few moments there I had the willies, but they didn't last." Sam flashed him a crooked smile. "Your voice helps keep me steady."

"Samantha." Her name was little more than a groan. "Don't say stuff like that while we're at work."

She had to laugh at his pained expression. "Okay, I won't."

When she would have pulled away, he shook his head. "You don't have to finish your Lifeline rotation. I'll talk to Jared if you like."

"Reese." She turned toward him, looking him directly in the eye. "I'm fine. Seriously. As soon as we dropped our patient off, I realized how lucky he was to have Lifeline there for him. The closest trauma center was easily forty minutes by ground transport. He never would have lasted that long." Her expression clouded. "He may not make it at all, but by us getting there so quickly he at least has a chance."

"But the person to put their life on the line doesn't have to be you," Reese argued.

She frowned. Was he worried about a repeat of what had happened to Valerie? "I'm only here for a few months, Reese. When I graduate, I'll get a staff position in an emergency trauma center someplace. I won't be flying anymore."

Instead of relief, his expression turned even more somber. She didn't know what to say to reassure him.

"I guess you'll just have to be my regular pilot," she teased lightly. "That way, you know I'll be in good hands."

Their pagers went off simultaneously before he could respond. "Car versus train, two victims in the car, both adults, but the woman is pregnant."

"Where's the peds crew?" Samantha asked, as they ran toward the helicopter. Lifeline maintained two choppers for just this reason, although the mother's life had to come first. "We don't know the viability of the fetus."

"On their way to Children's Memorial with a transport. They'll respond if we give them the word," Reese informed her. "Come on. Where's Andrew?"

"Right behind you, ace." Andrew plunked his helmet on his head. "Ready to roll."

Samantha laughed as she jumped in behind Andrew. Maybe working for some air medical transport company wouldn't be so bad if the crew were just like this. Certainly she'd suffered worse rotations before.

She listened as Reese went through his pre-flight check, then radioed the base. "Lifeline to base. We're ready for takeoff."

"Roger, Lifeline, you're clear to go. Winds are coming out of the east."

Samantha listened as Reese communicated with the paramedic base. This time she didn't experience any of the previous pre-flight jitters as Reese took off. Surely the feeling was normal after hearing about a crash so close to home.

The helicopter suddenly lurched hard to the right. If Sam hadn't been strapped in, she would have been smashed against the door.

Before she could cue her mike to ask Reese what

happened, his voice came through her headset, calm and clear.

"Mayday, mayday. We're going down for an emergency landing."

CHAPTER TWELVE

REESE fought to keep the stick steady, sweat dripping down along the inside of his helmet, burning his eyes. *Come on, keep it level.* If he didn't hold the chopper level, the tip of his blades might hit something, sending them crashing. They'd be goners for sure.

The paramedic base rattled off commands in his ear, but he couldn't hear what they were saying through the thundering beat of his heart. He gripped the controls so hard he was surprised the handle didn't break in two. No matter how hard he tried to keep the chopper level, it kept lurching to the right. Something, a bird maybe, must have hit them, causing damage on the right side. They were only a few hundred feet up—all he needed to do was get back down to the helipad.

Easier said than done. The wobbly motion of the helicopter was far from reassuring. He started his descent. The building was close, too close to the helipad for comfort. If he misjudged the lurching motion of the helicopter, they'd crash. Lowering the chopper, he stared at the controls, fighting to keep the lopsided motion to a minimum. Finally, he landed, hard. He instantly cut the rotation of the blades just as one of the skids beneath the chopper gave away, sending them sideways. The helicopter shuddered to a halt. For a moment he just sat there.

They'd made it down alive.

"Samantha? Andrew? Are you guys all right?" Reese struggled to get out of his harness, the awkward angle of the chopper making it difficult.

"Reese? We're okay." Samantha's voice was reassuringly steady. "Can't get the door open, though."

"Use your feet to kick out the window." Reese was forced to use the same maneuver to get out as well. He climbed out, thankful to see Samantha already out and on the ground.

"What in the hell did you do to my chopper?" Mitch roared from the doorway.

"Something hit us. Must have been a bird." Reese locked his knees to keep himself upright. But he couldn't hide his shaking hands as he reached toward Samantha. "Are you sure you're not hurt anywhere?"

"No, I'm fine." Samantha smiled and grasped his hands tightly. He wanted her in his arms, but she held him off. "Thanks for getting us down safely."

He almost hadn't, but didn't think it was prudent to mention that fact. Slowly, he released her. "We'll need to call the base."

"Yeah, I want to know where the second helicopter is," Samantha threw over her shoulder as she ran to the phone. "We need to respond to this call."

"What? Are you nuts?" Reese argued hotly. "We almost crashed."

Samantha ignored him. "Base, where's the second chopper? Tell them to hustle over to Lifeline. Our chopper is down and we need to respond to this call. One of the crew members will need to switch with me."

"Samantha, you don't need to go." Reese tried to reason with her once she hung up the phone. "Someone else can help the victims."

"Let's help Mitch get the chopper off the helipad. The second one is on its way." Samantha wasn't listening.

He wanted to shake her. "Mitch has already hauled the busted chopper inside. But listen to me. You don't need to respond to this call."

"Yes, Reese, I do. There are two injured people out there who need me. One of them is pregnant. There isn't anyone else to go."

Before he could think of another argument, he heard the second chopper approach. Within minutes the chopper landed. Samantha pulled on her helmet and waited, ready to race to the helicopter.

When she approached, one of the other team members, a guy she didn't know, jumped off, wordlessly agreeing to change places with her.

Reese wasn't letting her go alone. He rushed to the pilot's door and gestured his intention to ride along. Nate looked confused, but luckily the less senior pilot didn't argue.

Within moments Reese was seated in the copilot's seat, as Nate communicated to base his request to takeoff. Reese grabbed the armrests and held his breath, expecting the worst, as Nate lifted the chopper from the ground.

Jared wouldn't be happy with him, but he didn't care. Reese knew he was supposed to file a crash report on the hard landing, but as far as he was concerned the report would have to wait.

If Samantha intended to go to the crash scene, he would go with her. Even if flying made his stomach bubble like molten lava.

Samantha's palms were damp, and she wiped them on her flight suit as she took several steadying breaths. Flying so soon after the hard landing wasn't easy, but there wasn't any choice. If those people needed help, she intended to be there.

She was grateful someone named David had agreed to switch places with her. With Shelly on board, they had one adult responder and one pediatric one, a good balance in her opinion. Her only regret was that Reese wasn't the pilot.

Would Reese fly again after their near miss? She honestly didn't know. She knew she and Andrew owed their lives to Reese's expertise in avoiding a serious crash.

She kept quiet while Nate communicated with the base regarding the location of the train-versus-car crash. Shelly didn't know anything about the hard landing. The paramedic base had only relayed the information of how Reese's chopper was down and unavailable to fly. Sam decided now wasn't the time to fill Shelly in on the gory details, not while they were in flight. Instead, she concentrated on the task at hand. There would be plenty of time to fall apart later.

"ETA two minutes." Nate's nasal voice broke into her thoughts. "See that field over there? That's where I'm bringing her down."

Shelly nodded at her, indicating she agreed with

Nate's decision. Sam grabbed hold of her seat and held her breath as Nate settled the chopper on the ground with a gentle bump.

Samantha and Shelly jumped down, then went round the chopper to pull the gurney out from the hatch.

Sam surveyed the scene. The damage didn't look nearly as bad as it could have been. The car was smashed in on the rear bumper of the driver's side, but must have spun clear around as the front was wedged up against a tree. The paramedics on scene waved them forward.

"The driver is a male, he's the worst of the two. The woman is conscious, but she's trapped inside. She's also in active labor, crying that she feels the need to push. Has either of you ever delivered a baby?"

"I haven't helped deliver a baby since nursing school." Shelly's face was pale and her hand hovered over her own abdomen. Belatedly, Samantha remembered hearing about Shelly's pregnancy.

"I have," Samantha admitted as she swallowed hard. "I did a month's rotation in OB last year." She didn't add how delivering a baby in a controlled environment with the experts at hand was very different than managing the same task out in the field like this. She didn't have many options, from what she could see. "I'll take the mother."

"I'll look at the driver." Shelly didn't hide her relief.

"I'll give you a hand, Samantha." Reese's deep voice came from behind her.

She glanced at him, shocked to see him, but there wasn't time to ask why he'd come along. "Fine. The paramedics can help Shelly." Shelly specialized in peds, but with the paramedic's help she should be able to handle the driver. "Reese, give me a hand. We have to get her out of there or she'll be delivering that baby on her own."

Sam headed over to where a couple of firefighters were prying open the passenger door, Reese by her side.

"Almost got it," one of them grunted. With one last pull the door opened and fell to the ground.

Samantha crouched in the opening beside the sobbing woman. "I'm here. Everything's okay. You need to help me now, so we can save your baby." She sharpened her tone, trying to get through to the nearly hysterical woman. "How far apart are your contractions?"

"I don't know." The woman spoke between sobs. Sam was glad she was trying to cooperate. "Just before we crashed, they were five minutes apart. I don't have a watch, but they seem to be almost one right after the other."

Too close, that's exactly what Samantha had been afraid of. Any thoughts of loading her patient into the chopper and taking her directly to Trinity faded fast. "Are you hurt anywhere? Your neck? Your head? We need to get you out of this car."

"My head hurts a little, but nothing like these contractions," the woman gasped, and cried out. "I was in such pain, Eddie was rushing me to the hospital. He tried to beat the train, but it clipped our bumper, spinning us into the tree." The woman's face contorted. "How is Eddie? Oh, God, here's another one," she wailed as a contraction tightened her abdomen.

"Breathe through the pain, pant." Samantha wished she'd paid more attention during her OB rotation. When she'd assisted in delivering babies, the nurses had taken the role of coaches.

"Like this." Reese stepped up and demonstrated the technique, helping the woman breathe. Sam could barely hide her amazement. How did he know what to do?

"We need to turn her so I can examine her," Samantha told Reese in a low tone. "The baby is close."

Between them they got the woman turned in the seat enough that Sam could kneel on the grass in front of the passenger door and examine her patient. Sure enough, there was a round bulge where the baby's head was crowning.

There wasn't time to think. "All right, the next time you feel a contraction, I want you to push."

"Are you sure?" Reese's eyebrows rose.

"Yes, I'm sure. This baby isn't going to wait much longer." Sam tried to smile reassuringly at the woman. There weren't stirrups to use, so she hooked one of her patient's legs over her shoulder and propped the other on the rail of the paramedic's gurney. Without a fetal monitor, she could only hope and pray the baby was okay.

"I feel one coming." The woman tried to struggle into a sitting position.

"Reese, help her sit up, will you?"

He quickly obeyed, doing his best to anchor the patient's leg on the rail of the gurney before crawling in beside her, putting a hand beneath her back.

"Oh, God, it hurts," she whimpered.

"Push, come on, push hard." Samantha kept her hand over the top of the baby's head as the woman pushed. She heard Reese speaking to the woman in his low, husky voice reinforcing her need to push. Slowly, the head and face emerged. She gently guided the birth, turning the baby's head to the side and using her index finger to make sure the cord wasn't wrapped around the neck.

Thank heavens, she couldn't feel the cord. "Now push again. The baby is almost out, we only need to get past the shoulders. Come on, push." Samantha was grateful for Reese's help as he gave words of encouragement through the woman's sobs while she pushed.

Tiny shoulders emerged from the birth canal and the rest of the baby quickly followed. She felt Reese's awed gaze on her as Samantha held the tiny, slippery infant and quickly used the portable suction from their equipment pack to clear the baby's nose and mouth.

She didn't have time to do a full Apgar score, but guessed it to be in the six to seven range. As soon as she'd suctioned the mouth, the baby cried. Relief washed over her and sudden tears made her blink. "A boy. You have a beautiful baby boy."

"A boy!" The woman was sobbing in earnest now, but the radiant happiness on her features reassured

Sam that these were tears of joy. "Is he all right? Please, tell me he's going to be all right."

"He's fine. Listen to him cry," Reese said with a relieved smile. "He sounds like a healthy boy."

Samantha used the blanket from the gurney to wrap around the infant, then went to work on the umbilical cord. Using the string from a suture pack, she tied off the cord and cut it off with bandage scissors. They weren't sterile but clean enough, she hoped.

Birth was such a miracle. For long moments she and Reese could only gaze at the mother holding her baby. When his eyes, full of wonder, met hers, she had to fight another surge of tears. The expression in his gaze mirrored her thoughts. Thank heavens they'd gotten there when they had. The paramedics probably would have done fine, but her expertise, as little as it was, hadn't hurt.

After the placenta was delivered, she asked Reese for help in placing the woman on the gurney.

"How did you know what to do?" she couldn't help but ask, after making sure mother and baby were comfortable. "Have you assisted with deliveries before?"

"Sort of. I had to step in and help out my sister when she gave birth to my nephew, Adam, because her husband was stuck overseas and couldn't get back." Reese actually turned red. "Breathing was the only thing I remembered, the rest was a big blur. There are some things a brother shouldn't watch."

Samantha laughed. "Well, you helped tremendously. I'm so relieved they're both doing fine." With a guilty start she remembered their other patient. She turned toward the opposite side of the car. "Have you heard anything about the driver?"

"No."

"Stay here," Samantha directed, before going round the car and kneeling beside Shelly and a paramedic. "How is he?"

"He's not doing well." Shelly glanced up with a frown. "Heavy bleeding internally, I suspect. We can't get volume into him fast enough."

Of the two, the driver needed to get to hospital the fastest. Sam turned to the paramedic helping Shelly. "You guys need to take mom and baby to Trinity by ambulance. Reese? We need to take the driver in the chopper."

"Gotcha." The paramedic stood and headed back to where mother and baby were waiting. He quickly wheeled the gurney to the nearest waiting ambulance.

Samantha returned to the driver. Reese came to help them lift the male patient onto the Lifeline gurney. "Let's get airborne. We can pump fluids into him en route. The only thing that will help him now is getting into the OR."

With help from Reese's strong muscles, they hauled their patient through the field into the waiting chopper. Reese climbed in beside Nate. Sam instructed Shelly to keep pumping fluids and blood into their patient while they flew to Trinity. She couldn't imagine losing the woman's husband, Eddie. He needed to see his newborn son.

"Hang on, Eddie," she whispered, squeezing blood into him. "You have a son who needs you. Hang on."

"ETA four minutes," Nate informed them.

"Reese? Call Trinity and request they have an OR ready to go."

"Roger." She listened, keeping an eye on Eddie's blood pressure as Reese did as asked. By the time Nate landed, the ED crew was waiting for them. Within moments they rushed Eddie into the operating room, where the surgeons were ready to explore the patient's abdomen to find the source of bleeding.

Samantha felt her shoulders slump as the doors shut behind them. There was nothing more to do. Eddie's life was in good hands now. If the trauma surgeons at Trinity couldn't save him, no one could.

"Hey, I heard you delivered a boy." Shelly smiled, her hand once again hovering over her abdomen. "I'm so glad you were there. I don't think I could have delivered a baby."

She tried to smile. "Let's just hope he has a chance to know his dad."

"I know." Shelly's expression clouded and Sam wondered if she was thinking of the risks of her own career.

Sam knew they couldn't save all their patients; no one could. But, still, she couldn't imagine how that poor wife would feel to know she had lost her husband in the process of gaining a son.

Up on the helipad, Nate and Reese waited to take them back to Lifeline.

Samantha felt drained, too exhausted to feel nervous about flying. Shelly also remained quiet as they returned to Lifeline.

Jared was waiting for them on the helipad when

they landed. By the expression on his face, he wasn't happy.

Nate shut down the engines while everyone jumped out of the chopper. Shelly headed straight for her husband, giving him a brief hug. Jared returned the gesture, but his face remained grim.

"What's up?" Nate wanted to know.

"Jared?" Reese approached more slowly. "I know I need to do a crash report. I'll do it right now."

"A crash report?" Shelly echoed. "What happened?"

"A bird or something struck the chopper just as we were taking off. Reese had to bring us down in an emergency landing."

"Oh, my gosh." Shelly looked horrified. "I've read about others suffering hard landings, but I've never experienced one."

Sam grimaced. "We were fine, thanks to Reese, but you should see the chopper. It's in pretty bad shape."

"I'm not worried about the crash report." Jared finally spoke, his words slow and deliberate as his gaze encompassed all of them. "But you need to know, the chopper wasn't struck by a bird. Mitch found a bullet hole in the right-hand side of the engine. Someone shot at you."

A wave of nausea washed over her. "Someone shot at us? You mean, on purpose?" She glanced at Reese, afraid to verbalize her thoughts out loud.

Because the only person she could imagine doing such a terrible thing was Denis.

CHAPTER THIRTEEN

SAMANTHA stared at the round bullet hole Mitch obligingly showed her in the engine, trying to assimilate what the evidence so glaringly pointed out.

Had Denis really done this? Could he have gone that far over the deep end of reality?

Maybe there wasn't any evidence pointing to Denis as the culprit, but who else could it be? It wasn't as if Lifeline made a lot of enemies that the bullet would be the random act of some disgruntled customer. In the middle of February, in the heart of the city, there was no chance of a freak hunting accident. This had been an intentional shot.

The sick feeling in her stomach told her it was Denis. The smashed battery and the brick through her window already proved he was capable of violence. But this was worse. Much worse.

He'd almost killed the entire crew.

Think. She needed to think. "Have you notified the police?"

"Yeah. I've already given them a statement." Jared nodded toward the office. "They're waiting for both of you."

Reese fell into step beside her, but his dark gaze was difficult to read.

This mess was her fault, and she knew it. She'd caused Reese to relive his worst nightmare. They'd almost crashed—had, in fact, suffered a crash landing. Reese must have thought about ending up like Valerie a dozen times. She should have tried much harder to convince Jared to find a replacement for her. Her request for reassignment had been token at best. With Rafter's evidence, she'd honestly thought her problems with Denis were over.

Obviously not.

"Have they arrested Denis yet?" she asked as she and Reese made their way through the hangar toward Jared's office.

Jared shook his head. "No, and I gave them a piece of my mind about that. How difficult can it be for the entire Milwaukee Police Department to find one man?"

Samantha held her tongue. Denis had managed to slip through the fingers of the police for well over a year. Personally, she had more faith in Rafter's chances of bringing him in.

The door of Jared's office was open and there were two uniformed police officers seated inside. They stood when she and Reese entered.

When Reese remained close to her, she was glad. He had every right to be angry with her, but she knew his protective instincts well enough to know he'd stick with her until Denis was taken into custody. Guilt churned in her belly. Thanks to her, Reese had almost been killed. The thought made her sick.

"This is Dr Samantha Kearn." Jared introduced her to the officers. "We have good reason to suspect her ex-husband is the one who fired at the helicopter."

Sam recognized one of the officers as the same guy who'd come to investigate after the brick had been hurled through her bedroom window. She nodded at them in greeting.

"Dr Kearn, we have a few questions for you." The older of the two men indicated a vacant seat. "Please, sit down."

Because the trembling in her knees was so bad, she gratefully sat and folded her hands in her lap. "What can I help you with?"

"When was the last time you saw your ex-husband?" he wanted to know.

Sam tempered a flare of impatience. "I haven't actually seen him at all." She thought back over the flower delivery, the note under her door and brick through her window. Why did they think she'd spoken to him?

Wait a minute. She *had* seen Denis. Abruptly, she straightened in her seat. In the lobby of Trinity Medical Center she'd witnessed the brief meeting between Denis and her boss, Dr Ben Harris.

"No, that's not true," Sam admitted slowly. "I did see Denis, once, in the lobby at Trinity Medical Center."

"When?" Reese asked sharply.

She nearly winced. She hadn't intended to keep this a big secret. "The day I went to do Andrew's follow-up visits. I saw Denis. He was dressed in a very nice suit and he shook hands with Ben Harris."

"Harris? The medical director of Trinity's Emergency Department?" Jared asked.

"Yes. I was shocked when I saw them together,

especially because, technically, Dr Harris is my boss." She turned toward the officers. "Denis is a pharmaceutical sales rep. I assumed he was meeting with Dr Harris on business."

"Did Markowicz see you?" Reese's voice was low, vibrating with anger.

"I don't know." She remembered her quick dash across the lobby, trying to hide her face in the hood of her Lifeline jacket. "We'd just gotten a call for a transfer, so I bolted through the front door."

The older officer turned to Jared. "Where exactly is Dr Harris's office?"

Jared gestured through the small window. "In the medical staff office building—you can see the white building right there." The office building was adjacent to Trinity Medical Center for the convenience of the physicians.

"We need to speak to Dr Harris," the younger officer said.

"I'm coming with you." Sam quickly stood. She wanted to know for herself, too. Had she made things worse by not telling her boss the entire truth about Denis? She could imagine Denis setting up a meeting with Ben Harris, giving him a sob story of the aggrieved ex-husband trying to reconcile with his wife. Ben certainly knew about her divorce, if not the gory details.

Reese stayed with her as they all walked over to the medical staff office building. Jared led the way to the seventh floor, where all the ED staff physicians' offices were located.

"Grace, tell Dr Harris we need to see him," Jared

told the medical staff secretary, seated in the outer office. "It's important."

"I would, Dr O'Connor, but Dr Harris is in Chicago, attending a trauma lecture." Grace's eyes flickered between the group, noting the police officers standing behind Sam. "I can contact him, though."

"Go ahead. Or maybe you can help us." Jared stepped closer. "Do you know why Dr Harris met with Denis Markowicz?"

"Markowicz. Hmm. The name rings a bell." Grace went to work at the computer. "Oh, yes. I remember setting this meeting up. Denis Markowicz requested a meeting with Dr Harris regarding a business matter." She peered at them over the top of her glasses and shrugged. "I don't know anything more detailed, I'm afraid."

"Did Dr Harris often meet with sales reps?" Samantha asked.

"No, not often."

"Contact him for us," Jared instructed. "And can you let us into his office?"

"Sure." The woman hastily stood, grabbed a set of keys off her desk and led the way down the hall. "Dr Harris's office is the last one here, in the corner."

She opened the door and gasped, taking a step back when a blast of cold air hit. "Good heavens! The window is open."

Samantha edged inside, the sick feeling in her stomach twisting like a snake trying to get loose. The window was indeed wide open, but that wasn't what robbed her of speech. No, worse than the open window in the middle of winter was the fact that her boss's office directly overlooked Lifeline's helipad.

She barely listened as the questions started all over again.

"What time did you get in this morning?" The officers badgered Grace. "How long has Dr Ben Harris been gone?"

"He left yesterday, no, the day before." The poor woman wrung her hands in distress. "I came in at the usual time, eight-thirty this morning."

"We were in flight at half past seven," Reese told them. "The shot came minutes after takeoff."

"How did Markowicz get in? Was the office locked this morning?"

Grace shook her head miserably. "Not the main office area. The attending physician on duty in the ED usually comes in early, prior to the start of their shift. They open the general office area, drop off their stuff, then go down to work. The individual offices are locked, though," she added helpfully.

"He must have gotten in somehow." Jared sounded distinctly annoyed. "We need to find him before he succeeds in doing something far worse."

The officers agreed and more assistance was requested to record the potential crime scene. From what Sam could tell, Denis hadn't left any evidence other than the open window.

Reese pulled Sam and Jared aside. "We need to make some decisions about future flights. Maybe we should remain grounded until he's caught."

Samantha sucked in a quick breath. The idea of

refusing calls went against her nature. "Do you think that's necessary? He isn't here now."

"But we don't know where he is," Reese argued.

"I have to agree." Jared frowned. "All we can do is add pressure to get them to capture him quickly."

"I think it would be best to let me resign." Samantha couldn't stand to be the cause of more grief. "The repairs on the chopper will take a while anyway. You won't need two crews."

"I won't accept your resignation, but I agree you should remain grounded, at least until Markowicz is caught."

She'd find a way to resign, but sensed pushing Jared wasn't going to help. She risked a glance at Reese. "What about Reese? It's possible Denis saw us together." Her face flamed, but she held her head up high. She knew she should have stayed away from Reese, but she hadn't listened to the voice of reason. Instead, her desire to be with Reese had nearly killed them.

"Denis is possessive and controlling." She took a deep breath and let it out slowly. She couldn't bear to look at Reese. "I'm not sure, but I think his violence may have escalated because he saw us together down at the lakefront."

Reese inwardly swore, a vile word he hadn't used since his Air Force days. Dammit, he should have known something like this would happen. By trying to protect Samantha, he'd made things worse.

No, he hadn't made things worse by protecting her, but because he hadn't been able to keep his hands off her. The truth couldn't be denied. He'd crossed the line of friendship and, as a result, sent Markowicz into a frenzy.

He forced himself to remain calm. "I'll agree to remain grounded, but first I need to make a brief trip in the air." Flying alongside Nate wasn't quite the same as flying himself. He knew if he didn't get up with his hand at the stick soon, he'd lose his nerve.

Jared must have understood because he nodded. "Fine. Let's head back to Lifeline, then."

They made their way to the front part of the office. Grace waved at them, phone up to her ear. "Wait. Dr O'Connor? I have Dr Harris on the line."

Samantha put a hand on Jared's arm. "Let me speak to him."

Jared gestured for her to go ahead.

Reese listened intently to her one-sided conversation.

"Ben? It's Samantha Kearn. Why did you meet with Denis Markowicz the other day?" She fell silent, the corner of her mouth tugged down in a frown. "I see. I never thought he'd ask your personal advice about our divorce. I'm sorry, I should have told you I have a restraining order against him." Another pause, then she said, "I've tried to give my resignation to Dr O'Connor, but he won't accept it. Yes, I'll have him call you when you return. Thanks, Ben." She hung up the phone.

"Markowicz actually contacted your boss for advice on getting you back?" Reese couldn't believe what he'd heard.

Sam nodded. "I should have told Ben the truth up front, but I was too embarrassed."

He wanted to ask if she'd convinced her boss to find a replacement for her at Lifeline, but he was torn. On the one hand, he wanted her out of danger. The near miss this morning still rattled his bones. But on the other hand, the idea of losing Samantha was unthinkable.

But, then, once she left Lifeline and Markowicz was no longer a threat, she wouldn't need him anymore. He tried not to dwell on his own selfishness.

Back at Lifeline, Reese completed the rest of the paperwork surrounding the hard landing. The FAA would need to talk to him as well, he knew. Since the peds crew was out on a call, he didn't have the opportunity to take a chopper up, although they were expected back soon.

Either way, he wasn't sure he had it in him to fly. Riding beside Nate had been hard enough.

Samantha poked her head into the debriefing room. "I just called to check on our patients. Mom and baby are doing fine. Dad made it through surgery, but he's still in a critical condition."

More proof there were no guarantees. It dawned on him that if he married someday, his child could grow up without a father, too. With an effort he pushed aside his morbid thoughts.

"I'm ready to head home," Samantha told him.

"I'll come with you." He shoved his report aside.

She shrugged. "If you want, but I have my car here."

"I can drive you home." Reese couldn't bear to let her out of his sight. Not while Markowicz was still on the loose.

"I don't want to leave my car. Remember what happened last time?" Samantha's mouth was set in the familiar stubborn line. "You can follow me, if that makes you feel better."

It didn't, but since their apartment complex was only a few miles away, he figured it would have to do. "Fine, I'll follow you. But we're going to my place."

Sam's expression was troubled. He expected an argument, but she nodded. "I guess we should talk."

His gut clenched. Was this when she'd give him the brush-off? Thanks, it was fun, but since you almost got me killed, I think it's better if we don't see each other anymore?

With a grimace he knew he couldn't blame her. Silently he grabbed his coat, then held hers out for her, before heading outside.

The day was cloudy and cold. He waited until Sam was safe inside her car with the engine running, before heading to his.

He turned the key in the ignition, but his car wouldn't start. With a frown, he tried again. Dammit, how could his battery be dead? His lights turned off automatically and all his doors were closed.

The image of Samantha's hammer-smashed battery came to mind. With a curse he popped the hood and got out of his car. He waved at Samantha, indicating she should come over.

Instead, she simply looked at him, a strange expression in her eyes. She waved, then slowly drove away.

"Wait!" He started after her. The silhouette of a

second head appeared through the back window of her ancient Oldsmobile and his heart squeezed painfully.

Someone was in the car with her. Markowicz.

Reese didn't stop to think. He dashed inside Lifeline and shouted at Jared. "Call 911. Markowicz is in the back seat of Samantha's car."

Without waiting for a response, he went through the building to the hangar, then outside to the helipad. The second helicopter had just landed. Impatiently, he grabbed his helmet and gestured for Nate to get out.

Nate shut the engine down and jumped out. Reese snatched the key from his hand. "Hey, what're you doing?"

"I'm going up. Markowicz has Samantha." He jumped into the pilot's seat and started the engine. Communicating with the paramedic base wasted precious seconds, but he couldn't afford to lift off without them knowing. Heaven knew, they could accept a transfer from another helicopter transport company without realizing he was out there.

"Paramedic base, this is Lifeline informing you of takeoff." He buckled his harness with a snap. "I also need you to patch me through to the police."

"Roger, Lifeline, but where are you going?" The dispatcher sounded confused. "We aren't aware of a call."

"Patch me through to the police," Reese repeated. For a second he hesitated, then took a deep breath and lifted off. Banking left, he circled the area over the Lifeline parking lot and scanned the road below, searching for Samantha's car.

His heart hammered in his chest when he didn't see the familiar car. Then his gaze picked out a large burgundy-colored vehicle just under a mile away from the parking lot. The car seemed to be moving deliberately slower than the rest of the traffic, heading away from the city on a small highway rather than the interstate. There were other cars, but Samantha's older-model car had a bulky frame that stood out from the rest.

"Found you," he whispered in satisfaction. "Base, do you have the police yet? I'm following Dr Samantha Kearn's vehicle west on Highway 20. Denis Markowicz is suspected to be inside."

"You're using the helicopter to follow someone?" The dispatcher's voice rose in alarm. "That's not allowed."

Reese gnashed his teeth. "All the more reason to put me through to the police. Now!" They could call out the entire National Guard as far as he was concerned. Samantha was in trouble. He didn't care how help arrived.

"All right, I hear you." The dispatcher paused, then came back on the radio, "Go ahead, the police are on the same frequency. Officer, you're on." The dispatcher finally turned the mike over to the police.

"You have the suspect in sight? What's the make of the vehicle?" the police officer wanted to know.

"A burgundy Oldsmobile, heading west on Highway 20." Reese hovered over Samantha's car, wishing he could do more. "I don't know the license-plate number."

"And you're certain Markowicz is inside?" the officer questioned.

There was no doubt in Reese's mind that he had seen two figures in the car. Since Samantha had gone to her car alone, he figured Markowicz must have been hiding in the back seat. Was he sure enough to stake her life on it? "Yes, I'm certain."

"When they get out of the city, we'll set up a roadblock," the officer told him. "Keep the car in sight."

"I will." There was no way he'd lose her now.

The palms of his hands were sweaty on the stick, but Reese couldn't afford the luxury of being nervous. He had to keep an eye out for possible birds, flying high enough to be out of the way of treacherous phone lines and at the same time making sure he wasn't so high he lost Samantha.

He absolutely refused to lose her ever again.

Up ahead, he could see a long stretch of highway, relatively free of traffic. Sure enough, there were several police cars setting up the promised roadblock.

"Hang on, Samantha," he prayed. With a wide sweeping curve, he came back round, keeping the burgundy car in sight. "Officer, I see the roadblock. The suspect's car is headed directly toward it."

"Ten-four. We have a sharpshooter in position to take out the vehicle's tires," the officer replied.

"What?" Reese shouted, his hand swerving on the stick. He quickly straightened the chopper. "What if she crashes?"

"We need to get this car off the road. I've been

told there's a possibility the suspect has weapons in his possession.''

He didn't doubt Markowicz had the gun he'd used to shoot down the chopper. Reese swallowed his protest. Samantha was cool under pressure, he'd seen her in action more than once. She'd saved countless lives while flying thousands of feet in the air. She wouldn't crash. She'd be fine.

Dear God, please, let her be fine.

As if watching a movie in slow motion, he saw her vehicle slow dramatically, then swerve wildly on the road when a tire blew out. He held his breath until the car slowed to a wobbly stop, then desperately sought a close place to land.

He decided the stretch of highway that the cops had conveniently blocked off would have to do. Without sparing more than a passing thought to the last time he'd landed, he lowered the chopper down onto the concrete road.

After shutting down the engine, he jumped out. Samantha's car was just twenty yards away. He heard cops shouting at him but didn't listen.

Then he saw her and his boots congealed like tar, stopping him in his tracks. Samantha's car door opened, and she emerged from the inside with Markowicz at her side, holding a knife to her throat.

CHAPTER FOURTEEN

SAMANTHA saw Reese, wanted to run straight toward him, but she didn't dare breathe when Denis whispered, "You didn't come back. Why not? Because of lover boy over there?"

Oh, God, she didn't know what to do. Denis seemed beyond reason. Reese was so close yet she didn't dare acknowledge him for fear Denis would turn his wrath on him.

Stall. She needed more time.

"We're surrounded," she began, but when the knife he held pressed closer, she clamped her mouth shut. For support she held on to the arm he'd wrapped around her neck as he forced her to walk forward. He wouldn't listen to reason anyway. Bile rose in her throat, threatening to choke her. The entire time he'd been in the car, he'd kept trying to convince her everything was her fault.

Just a few short hours ago she might have believed him. It was her fault she'd married him, but that was the extent of it. Seeing Denis now, she realized she wasn't in charge of his actions.

No one was but him. It was time he faced the truth.

"Tell them you made a mistake," he hissed in her ear. Slowly, he turned her in a circle so that everyone could see the knife he held to her throat. "Tell them you're my wife and your place is home with me. Tell them!''

Sam bit back a cry, her grip on his arm slipping when his hand tightened.

''Tell them this is all your fault. You should never have left me, Sammie. You never should have left.''

She shivered, his whispered voice haunting her, flooding her with memories of the past. How many times had she listened to similar taunts? The familiar lethargy seeped through her pores, sapping her will to fight. She suspected Denis would rather kill her than give up to the police.

Her gaze settled on Reese standing statue still while he stared at her, his gaze imploring her to hang on. Suddenly she knew Reese would risk his life for her.

The thought snapped the invisible hold Denis wielded. Reese had faced his fears, flying the helicopter to find her. She deserved a normal life, and she was damned if she let Denis control her another second.

She sent Reese a warning glance, trying without words to tell him what she was about to do. She tightened her grasp on Denis's arm then stomped on his foot, at the same time pushing with all her strength against his arm. Denis wasn't used to her fighting back. For a second he yelped in pain and loosened his grip, just enough so she could tear herself free.

She ran straight toward Reese, who simultaneously sprinted toward her. He caught her up in his arms and held her close. There was a stampede of movement behind her, shouts from several officers and just that quickly Denis was under arrest.

"You're safe, Samantha. Thank God, you're safe," Reese murmured against her hair.

She buried her face in his shoulder, breathed in his scent and sobbed. She knew, without looking, that the police had taken custody of Denis. He was probably still trying to blame everything on her, but this time they wouldn't listen.

He would be held accountable for his own actions.

It was finally over.

Reese was glad Samantha didn't need to spend too much time with the police. They'd found a rifle in the back seat of her car and had seized the weapon, suspecting it was the one used to shoot at the chopper.

He held on to Samantha's hand, unwilling to let her go as she finished her statement. When she was ready to go, he steered her toward the helicopter he'd left sitting in the middle of the road.

"I couldn't believe it when I saw you land this thing," Samantha confessed. "Were you following me the whole time?"

"Yeah." Reese knew the memory of what had nearly happened would stay with him forever. Reluctantly he released her hand and opened the chopper door. "I lost ten years off my life when I saw him through the back window of your car. I'm sorry, Samantha."

She raised a brow then plunked her helmet on her head. "Sorry for what? I insisted on driving separately, if you recall. And now that it's over, I'm glad. Denis is finally in custody. He can't control me anymore."

Reese fell silent as he put his helmet on, then gestured for her to get into the front seat. He was very glad her ex couldn't torment her ever again, but at the same time his usefulness was over. She didn't need his protection anymore.

And in a few more months Samantha would graduate from her emergency medicine residency and take her boards. He had no doubt she'd pass, then she'd head out to San Diego, three thousand miles from Wisconsin.

His heart squeezed painfully in his chest. Ignoring his sense of loss, he communicated with the paramedic base, explaining he was about to take off and return to Lifeline. He imagined the dispatcher was dying to know what had happened, but she simply gave him the go-ahead.

"Everything is so beautiful from up here." Samantha gazed in awe.

He didn't comment, but silently agreed. He could appreciate how the chopper had helped save Samantha from harm. Safety would always be his top concern, but he'd taken steps to ensure that would be the case for the rest of the crew.

It was time he stopped dwelling on the "what-ifs" of the past and focused his attention on the future.

Back at Lifeline, they found Jared pacing the length of the hangar.

"Dammit, Jarvis! What the hell kind of stunt was that?"

Reese straightened his spine but refused to apologize. "I understand your anger. But Samantha's life was in danger."

Jared blew out a long breath. "I'm glad you're okay, Samantha," he told her, before turning back toward Reese. "But you're not a cop, for Pete's sake. What were you thinking?"

"I was thinking about Samantha." Reese stood his ground. If Jared wanted to turn him over to the authorities, so be it. "I understood the risks and would take them again if need be."

Samantha frowned and reached out to place a hand on Jared's arm. "What risks? Jared, Denis was hiding in the back seat of my car. He must have made a spare set of keys while we were still married. Reese was only trying to look out for me."

"I know." Jared reached up and yanked on his hair with both hands, as if to pull the strands right out of his head. "Damn, this place is driving me nuts. I have a board of directors to answer to. I'll give you this one, Jarvis. We'll write this trip off as your way of getting back in the air after the forced landing. But don't try this stunt again."

"I'm not planning to," Reese said.

Samantha tugged on Jared's arm. "Do you have a minute? I need to talk to you about something."

"Sure." Resigned, Jared's anger deflated into a puff of smoke. He spun on his heel and headed toward his office. Samantha and Reese followed.

Samantha sent him a questioning look. "I'm fine, Reese. You don't need to stay glued to my side."

The dread in his gut spread like aviation fuel mixing with water. "I didn't realize you needed to talk to Jared in private." He couldn't help his tone sounding stiff, formal.

Her expression softened. "It's nothing like that. You can come if you like."

He wasn't reassured but couldn't bring himself to leave. In Jared's office, she went straight to the point. "I need a favor. I've decided not to continue in emergency medicine after I graduate."

What? Reese stared at her. She loved her job. Her ex was finally out of the picture. What was she talking about?

"What do you need from me?" Jared asked, his forehead furrowed in concern.

"A recommendation for placement in the critical care fellowship program." She spoke in a rush. "I've decided I don't like handing over the care of my patients to the critical care team. I need a more active part in making them well."

Jared's eyebrows rose. "You'll probably need an extra year of medical residency to qualify," he warned her. "Plus, the fellowship is for three years. On the other hand, they have positions to fill. You stand a good chance in landing one here."

"I know." Samantha's face practically glowed. "I've spent too much time wondering about how my patients are doing. And this is probably something I should have done long ago."

Reese couldn't believe what he was hearing. He should have been elated by her news, but he couldn't shake the inward feeling of alarm. If Samantha was staying, he had a chance at a real relationship. A possible future. Marriage. A home. Children.

All the things he'd once planned with Valerie.

He swallowed hard. Now that the coast was clear,

he hesitated on the edge of the cliff, unable to jump. What if he committed himself to Samantha, only to lose her anyway?

"Reese?" Samantha waved a hand in front of his eyes, her voice full of concern. "Are you all right? Maybe you should sit down."

"I'm fine." His voice was faint, as if he were talking through the thickness of his helmet. He cleared his throat and tried again. "What about San Diego?"

Her eyes widened in surprise. "San Diego?" she echoed.

"Yeah. Your family lives there." He felt foolish, but pressed on. "I overheard you talking to Jared about moving back home once you graduated."

"I didn't realize you knew about that." Samantha tilted her head quizzically, then shrugged a shoulder. "I don't want to leave," she said simply. "I want to stay here, in Milwaukee."

Panic swished and sloshed like a half-empty rain barrel in his chest. "You do?"

Her questioning gaze turned into a wounded one and he knew his reaction wasn't what she'd hoped to hear. Still, she squared her shoulders and glanced away. "Yes, I do. I have friends here. I don't want to leave."

Reese fell silent. Samantha had bravely fought against Markowicz and won. Did he possess the same bravery to fight against the ghosts in his past? To love again, without any guarantee of forever?

Samantha stood in front of her closet, trying to decide what to wear. Jared had called a few hours earlier, asking her to attend the Children's Memorial Hospital fund-raiser ball in his place because Shelly was sick. She'd agreed to go, although she wasn't in the mood to celebrate.

She hadn't seen Reese in days, since they'd both been grounded. Now that Denis wasn't a threat, she suspected their schedules wouldn't match.

Not that it should matter either way. She needed to finish these last few months at Lifeline. Going into critical care was the right decision for her career. She probably would have made the switch much sooner if she'd been thinking clearly. So what if her goal of being a physician was put off for another couple of years? She had the rest of her life.

A life that obviously didn't include Reese. The back of her eyes ached with the effort to hold back tears. He'd known about her plan to move to San Diego after graduation. Clearly he'd become intimate with her thinking their relationship was temporary.

No surprise. She suspected he was still hung up on Valerie.

She should have understood. Reese wasn't the type of guy to fall in love easily. Still, she'd hoped…

Never mind. She should be happy that Denis was in jail and she had her life back. Ridiculous to ask for anything more.

With a sigh she pulled out the only really formal dress she owned, a long black velvet dress that clung to her figure with a slit that showed off her legs when she walked. An eye-catching dress, but she wore it without enthusiasm.

She quickly put on a little makeup and fluffed her

hair, leaving it down to wave around her shoulders. A glance at her watch made her grab a wool shoulder wrap and head for the door.

Jared had mentioned something about a car picking her up, but she was stunned to see a stretch black limo parked outside her apartment building. When she stepped outside a driver, dressed sharply in black, jumped out to open the door for her.

"Thank you." She slid into the seat and glanced around in awe. She didn't mind being spoiled but somehow her sense of loneliness only increased sitting in the expansive back seat. A limo ride was something to be shared.

Her heart ached, wishing Reese could love her, but she'd been down that road once before. Denis hadn't loved her either. He'd been obsessed with controlling her, had been jealous of her success in a career he'd failed in, but he hadn't loved her.

She pushed thoughts of Reese aside and tried to enjoy her brief foray in luxury.

The limo driver let her out in front of the Milwaukee Art Museum, which overlooked Lake Michigan in downtown Milwaukee. The building was unique, inside and out. Samantha clutched her wrap and gazed around the expansive glass and marble foyer.

A discreet host took her wrap when she introduced herself, telling him she was representing Dr Jared O'Connor from Lifeline Medical Air Transport.

"We're pleased to have you here, Dr Kearn. May I get you something to drink?"

"A glass of Chardonnay, thank you."

Samantha gazed around the room, searching for a familiar face. When she didn't find anyone she knew, she took a sip of her wine and escaped the crowd by heading down the corridor to a special Vincent van Gogh exhibit.

The impressive paintings on the walls reflected her pensive mood. How long since she'd taken the time to appreciate art? She paused before a breathtaking scenic painting, *The Bridge at Trinquetaille*.

"Nice, but not nearly as beautiful as you."

Samantha started at the familiar male voice behind her. Warily she turned.

"Hello, Reese." She could barely get the greeting past the constriction in her throat. He was impressively handsome in a tux, seemingly as at home in formal wear as he was in his navy blue flight suit. "I didn't expect to see you here."

"Jared asked me to come in his place. He must have asked you, too."

"Yes." She raised a brow. "You didn't get a limo ride, though."

He tucked his hands in his pockets. "Maybe you'll share with me on the ride home."

She hesitated, then nodded, already missing the easy companionship she'd shared with him during their flights. The awkwardness between them now was painful. "Of course."

"I'd like to talk to you for a moment. Have a seat." She did as he asked, but the somber expression on his face made her heart plummet. Did Reese feel he needed to give her the brush-off in person? Because, if so, she could save him the trouble.

"Samantha, there's so much I need to explain to you. About me. About Valerie."

She tensed, not sure she wanted to hear this. She'd only been in his apartment once, but even then, she couldn't remember seeing any pictures of his fiancée. In fact, the thing that had struck her had been how much his décor matched hers by being totally absent.

No pictures of him and his fiancée hung on the walls. No personal knick-knacks sat on tables. There was no evidence of his previous life. With a frown she wondered if he kept a picture of Valerie in his bedroom. Or had he locked all the visual reminders away deep in his heart?

"You don't need to explain anything to me, Reese. Really, I understand. I know what you're trying to tell me."

"You do?" He looked shocked by her admission.

With a sense of defeat she nodded. He had come after her when Denis had grabbed her. It was only fair she let him off the hook now. "We became close under rather bizarre circumstances and things moved quickly. Too quickly."

"Marry me."

She blinked. "Excuse me?"

There was a hint of laughter in his eyes. "I thought you knew what I was going to say? Well, this is it. I'm asking if you would, please, marry me."

Stunned, she stared at him. "But…I thought…you were so…"

Reese dropped beside her on the bench seat, took her hand in his and slipped a modest diamond ring on her finger. "This ring belonged to my grandmother, but you can choose another if you'd prefer. I've been thinking about us, about the future. You are so amazing Samantha, so courageous. I wish I could say the same for me, but I'm slow. It took me a while to admit I've been running from commitment because I was afraid of losing you."

"I'm not lost," she whispered.

"I know." He smiled and her heart simply melted. "I'm not lost anymore either. What I had with Valerie was precious, but it also wasn't meant to be. I love you, Samantha. More than I ever thought I'd love anyone again." He cleared his throat. "I know there aren't any guarantees but I'll take whatever time we're given. Life was meant to be shared with someone you love."

"Oh, Reese." She didn't know what to say.

"Will you, please, marry me?" His gaze was serious on hers.

She couldn't imagine a more beautiful proposal. For a moment she gazed down at his grandmother's ring. The setting was dainty, with a dazzling center stone. She could hardly believe he cared enough to give her his grandmother's ring. Her eyes misted and she lifted her gaze to his.

"I love you, too, Reese. I learned being with you gives me strength. When you came after me in the Lifeline helicopter, I realized I wanted to fight for a chance at love."

Reese tugged her off the seat and into his arms. His hands splayed over her velvet dress, pressing her along his hard length. "Build a life with me." He kissed her. "Have children with me." He kissed her again. "Let's live every day to the fullest." He kissed her a third time, lingering over her mouth.

Surrendering her heart to Reese was easy, for he gave her his in return. A true partnership. Everything she'd always wanted.

"Yes." She smiled through her tears. "Starting now and for the rest of our lives."

Medical romance

HOLDING OUT FOR A HERO
by Caroline Anderson (The Audley)

Five years ago Ben Maguire was a brilliant doctor – now he's a daring and courageous TV presenter. In the latest episode of *Unsung Heroes*, he must follow the fast-paced life of beautiful A&E nurse Meg Fraser. She can't help noticing that he freezes at the first sign of an emergency, but the chemistry sizzles between them – and Ben knows he can't hide the truth from her for ever...

HIS UNEXPECTED CHILD by Josie Metcalfe
(The ffrench Doctors)

Helping couples become parents brings delight to Leah Dawson – especially as she cannot carry a baby to full term herself. Leah gives everything to her work, and she's infuriated when promotion is taken from her by the gorgeous Dr David ffrench. But the special care he takes with his patients is enough to steal her heart, and their relationship deepens...

WHERE THE HEART IS by Kate Hardy (24/7)

The stunning glacial peaks of Patagonia seem the perfect place for Dr Rowena Thompson to heal her emotions. But when she meets consultant Luke MacKenzie she learns that hers isn't the only heart in need of help. They find a love that neither has experienced before – a love that is tested when Rowena faces a life-changing diagnosis...!

On sale 5th August 2005

Available at most branches of WHSmith, Tesco, ASDA, Martins, Borders, Eason, Sainsbury's and all good paperback bookshops

Visit www.millsandboon.co.uk

MILLS & BOON®

Live the emotion

Medical romance™

A FAMILY WORTH WAITING FOR

by Margaret Barker *(French Hospital)*

Jacky Manson can't believe it when her new post at the Hôpital de la Plage brings her face to face with Pierre Mellanger, the man she has loved ever since she can remember. At last he sees her for the beautiful and competent woman she is – but they both have secrets to reveal…and it's only in the telling that their lives will take a whole new turn!

IN HIS TENDER CARE **by** *Joanna Neil*

(A&E Drama)

Sasha Rushford balances an intense career as a paediatrician with her role as head of the family – she's used to calling the shots and going it alone. Her new boss, consultant Matt Benton, soon realises she is as much in need of saving as the children in their care – and he's determined to persuade her to accept the love he wants more than anything to give her.

EARTHQUAKE BABY **by** *Amy Andrews*

Trapped under a collapsed building, Laura Scott thought she would never survive. One man kept her alive and led her to safety – Dr Jack Riley. That life-saving moment led to a night of unforgettable intimacy, but it's ten years before they meet again. Jack soon discovers how real their connection was – and that Laura is the mother of a ten-year-old child…

On sale 5th August 2005

Available at most branches of WHSmith, Tesco, ASDA, Martins, Borders, Eason, Sainsbury's and all good paperback bookshops

Visit www.millsandboon.co.uk

MILLS & BOON®
Live the emotion

Love in the City

*Feeling **hot** in the city tonight…*

In August 2005, By Request brings back three favourite romances by our bestselling Mills & Boon authors:

Marriage in Peril by Miranda Lee
Merger by Matrimony by Cathy Williams
The Inconvenient Bride by Anne McAllister

Make sure you buy these passionate stories, on sale from 5th August 2005

Available at most branches of WHSmith, Tesco, ASDA, Martins, Borders, Eason, Sainsbury's and all good paperback bookshops.

www.millsandboon.co.uk

2 FULL LENGTH BOOKS FOR £5.99

No.1 *New York Times* bestselling author

NORA ROBERTS

"Exciting, romantic, great fun."
—Cosmopolitan

SUSPICIOUS

PARTNERS and *NIGHT MOVES*

On sale 15th July 2005

Available at most branches of WHSmith, Tesco, ASDA, Martins, Borders, Eason, Sainsbury's and all good paperback bookshops.

M011/M&E

MIRA
An international collection of bestselling authors

Narrated with the simplicity and unabashed honesty of a child's perspective, *Me & Emma* is a vivid portrayal of the heartbreaking loss of innocence, an indomitable spirit and incredible courage.

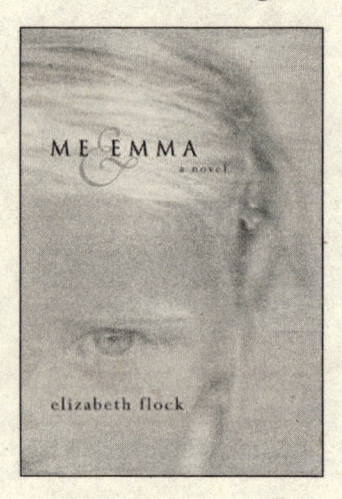

ME & EMMA

a novel

elizabeth flock

ISBN 0-7783-0084-6

In many ways, Carrie Parker is like any other eight-year-old—playing make-believe, dreading school, dreaming of faraway places. But even her naively hopeful mind can't shut out the terrible realities of home or help her to protect her younger sister, Emma. Carrie is determined to keep Emma safe from a life of neglect and abuse at the hands of their drunken stepfather, Richard—abuse their momma can't seem to see, let alone stop.

On sale 15th July 2005

4 FREE

BOOKS AND A SURPRISE GIFT!

We would like to take this opportunity to thank you for reading this Mills & Boon® book by offering you the chance to take FOUR more specially selected titles from the Medical Romance™ series absolutely FREE! We're also making this offer to introduce you to the benefits of the Reader Service™—

- ★ FREE home delivery
- ★ FREE gifts and competitions
- ★ FREE monthly Newsletter
- ★ Exclusive Reader Service offers
- ★ Books available before they're in the shops

Accepting these FREE books and gift places you under no obligation to buy, you may cancel at any time, even after receiving your free shipment. Simply complete your details below and return the entire page to the address below. You don't even need a stamp!

YES! Please send me 4 free Medical Romance books and a surprise gift. I understand that unless you hear from me, I will receive 6 superb new titles every month for just £2.75 each, postage and packing free. I am under no obligation to purchase any books and may cancel my subscription at any time. The free books and gift will be mine to keep in any case.

M5ZED

Ms/Mrs/Miss/Mr .... Initials ....

BLOCK CAPITALS PLEASE

Surname ....

Address ....

....

.... Postcode ....

Send this whole page to:
UK: FREEPOST CN81, Croydon, CR9 3WZ

Offer valid in UK only and is not available to current Reader service subscribers to this series. Overseas and Eire please write for details. We reserve the right to refuse an application and applicants must be aged 18 years or over. Only one application per household. Terms and prices subject to change without notice. Offer expires 31st October 2005. As a result of this application, you may receive offers from Harlequin Mills & Boon and other carefully selected companies. If you would prefer not to share in this opportunity please write to The Data Manager, PO Box 676, Richmond, TW9 1WU.

Mills & Boon® is a registered trademark owned by Harlequin Mills & Boon Limited.
Medical Romance™ is being used as a trademark. The Reader Service™ is being used as a trademark.